Cover Copy

He must steal a lady...then steal her love.

Desiring a man and never being noticed as more than his best friend's little sister has Lady Ellie Trentbury finally consigning herself to the truth. She must move on, and preferably with a man who lives far away from her home in London where she need never be reminded of the duke who stole her heart. An elopement with an honorable American shipping merchant sounds perfect.

The Duke of Ashten has no choice but to bound into his best friend's carriage when he discovers little Ellie is inside and intent on eloping with a man to Gretna Green who she barely knows. He can't allow her to make such a terrible mistake, yet convincing her might mean giving into his desire for the golden-eyed enchantress who has followed him around since he was a lad.

Her pouty lips and bountiful charms can no longer be ignored, only convincing her of the truth of his intentions will mean jeopardizing both his sanity and a lifelong friendship as well.

Books by Joanne Wadsworth

Books by Joanne Wadsworth

Regency Brides Series

The Duke's Bride, Book One
The Earl's Bride, Book Two
The Wartime Bride, Book Three
The Earl's Secret Bride, Book Four
The Prince's Bride, Book Five
Her Pirate Prince, Book Six
Chased by the Corsair, Book Seven

Princesses of Myth Series

Protector, Book One
Warrior, Book Two
Hunter (Short Story - Included in Warrior, Book Two)
Enchanter, Book Three
Healer, Book Four
Chaser, Book Five

The Duke's Bride

Regency Brides, Book One

JOANNE WADSWORTH

The Duke's Bride
ISBN-13: 978-1-54866-090-1
ISBN-10: 1-54866-090-6
Copyright © 2017, Joanne Wadsworth
Cover Art by Joanne Wadsworth
First electronic publication: August 2017

Joanne Wadsworth
http://www.joannewadsworth.com

AUTHOR'S NOTE:
This book is a work of fiction. The names, characters, places, and incidents are products of the writer's imagination or have been used fictitiously and are not to be construed as real. Any resemblance to persons, living or dead, actual events, locale or organizations is entirely coincidental. The author does not have any control over and does not assume any responsibility for third-party websites or their content.

Published in the United States of America

First digital publication: August 2017
First print publication: July 2017

Chapter 1

Blackgale House, London, 1810.

"Let me in, Ashten, this very instant." Lady Ellie Trentbury rapped on the Duke of Ashten's bedchamber door for the tenth time in ten minutes. "You are being obstinate, and since my brother would never allow this stubborn behavior of yours to continue, then neither shall I."

"Go away, Ellie. You're being a pest, yet again." One fierce growl rumbled from the other side of the paneled oak door along with the decided thump of pacing footsteps.

"I will leave once we've spoken, and not a moment before." She pulled a pin from her upswept chignon, stuck it into the lock on the duke's bedchamber door and jiggled it about. She wouldn't allow her brother's closest confidant to wallow in his grief yet another day, not while she still had breath in her body.

"What the blazes are you doing now?" The lock clicked and the door swung wide. Ashten's piercing blue gaze narrowed on her. "Do you even realize how improper your actions are?"

"Scandalous is more like it, but at least I now have your attention, and your door open." Hands clutched in the skirts of her burgundy day gown, she stormed past him and tossed her reticule on the gold and blue silk covers gracing his monstrous bed. "You might want to close your door. I wouldn't want your

7

staff to know I was in here."

"I imagine they'll guess since you've stopped shouting and demanding entrance." He left the door open and hands on his hips, towered over her. "Speak now and then leave."

"Lady Ashley never wished to wed a powerful duke. All she ever desired was to live a life of adventure on the seas, and she eloped with Captain Seymore for that very reason. You must cease blaming yourself for the decision she made to sail away." She grasped his jacketed arm. "Do you understand?"

"She is dead now because of me, gone to a watery grave within the very seas she wished to experience that adventure upon."

"It's been months and even though I still grieve for her too, we must move on." She gentled her tone and tried to blow away the loose golden tendril that had fallen in front of her eyes when she'd pulled her pin free. "Ashley had feared you were mere days away from proposing and since her father would have accepted your offer and never have allowed her to wed Seymore as she'd hoped, then she eloped to ensure the life she desired."

"Your Grace, is all well?" Gorman stood in the doorway, the silvery streaks at the sides of his dark-haired head glimmering in the firelight.

"You allowed Lady Ellie into the house when I expressly forbid you to never allow her entrance again."

Ashten's butler cringed and rubbed his chest. "Yes, but I can explain why. I could hardly—"

"There is no excuse. Now be gone." Ashten slammed the door shut with a gust of wind then stormed back to her. "You've done it now, entered the lion's den."

"Whatever you do, please don't punish Gorman for my actions." She tapped the pointed end of her parasol against his shoulder. "I pushed past him to gain entrance, and with a strike from my brolly he didn't see coming."

"I will punish him however I please, and Gorman doesn't

need you defending him." He plucked her parasol from her hand and tossed it on top of his bed. "I've seen him warding off men at the door with an actual weapon in hand, not a flimsy parasol."

"You have men wielding weapons at your door?" She gasped. Surely such a thing hadn't happened on this fine street he lived on. "Please tell me that is not true."

"On occasion, yes." He crossed his arms with a slap. "If you're caught here, Ellie, Winterly will certainly have you wed to me before you can utter a word in your defense. I know you've no desire for such a union between us. I certainly don't wish for one."

"Then it's just as well Winterly isn't here." He believed she had no desire? Ashten had always been blind to her and her feelings for him. She was naught more than his best friend's little sister, and always would be. Sadly, a fact she'd come to finally accept the day she'd learnt of his intention to propose to one of her dearest friends. Stiffening her spine, she composed herself and forced her emotions aside. "Ashley truly adored Seymore, and the storm which sank his vessel wasn't one you conjured up. That you can't argue with."

"I'm a duke and she was to be my duchess. My pursuit of her forced her hand." Gritting his teeth, he stepped up to her and she backed up, knocked her back against his carved bedpost and shoved one hand against his chest. "It's best I remain here in seclusion," he continued through gritted teeth. "So, I might never force the hand of another innocent lady again."

"I should have warned you about Ashley's feelings for Seymore and her impetuous nature. You also can't scare me away with your anger and domineering ways." She knew his heart, and no matter the current grief and guilt consuming him, she intended on bringing him back into the world of the living. "You can't remain a recluse forever. You haven't even stepped outside of Blackgale House since Ashley's death."

"My movements are of no concern of yours." He caught her

elbow, drew her across to the blue settee next to a mahogany side table holding a decanter and glasses and motioned for her to take a seat. Once she had, he poured a finger of amber liquid into a glass and swigged it down.

"Mama worries over you, and so do Sophia and Olivia."

"Your mama worries over everyone, from the milkmaid to the—"

"Harry mightn't be here anymore, but that doesn't exclude you from being a part of my family. I worry over you too."

"I neither want your sympathy, worry, or your interference. You're meddling into my affairs, and it isn't desired."

"I like meddling." She offered him a teasing smile, hoping to bring a smidgeon of relief to the tense moment. "Even Winterly worries over you. He told me so himself." Her eldest brother, the Earl of Winterly, had come into his title following their papa's death five years past.

"Honesty, Ellie, you need to put me out of your mind."

"I can't do that. They're calling you a murderer, and I won't have it." Anger throbbed fierce and tight in her chest. No one cared more for others than Ashten did. He'd gone to war to ensure those here in England remained safe in their homes. She owed him her life, as did everyone else within the *ton*. "Your self-isolation speaks of guilt. If you could just attend an event here or there within Society, it would help."

"I am a murderer," he stated tersely as he dropped down onto the settee beside her. "Lady Ashley perished because of me, although she is only one of many. A man loses his very heart and soul when having to wield a pistol and saber in times of war."

"You're no longer on the front line."

"Only due to my inability to remain out of the path of cannon fire. Napoleon holds France and is doing his damnedest to take Spain. Thousands of innocent men, women, and children are perishing in this war of atrocity."

"There is so much suffering." Too much, and she

desperately wished she could do more to halt it.

"Yet here I am," he continued with a grating tone, "still shedding blood even though not on the battlefield. The moment I attempted to return to Society, I caused the death of an innocent lady. That's unacceptable, Ellie, and must stop. If that requires I remain in seclusion for the remainder of my days, then so be it. You must accept that, just as I have."

"You have one of the kindest hearts of anyone I know, are no murderer at all." This man had stood by Harry's side, never forsaking her brother, not once during the seven years they'd spent away together at war. Heart throbbing, she lifted one hand and gently set it on his cheek. She traced her fingers over the scar disappearing into his hairline. "I miss Harry."

"I miss him too, but he'll return once this damned war is done. He'd better." He heaved away, seating himself in the gold-patterned cushioned wingchair across from her. "You shouldn't have come, even though you felt driven to."

"I've missed you as well." She couldn't lose him, not now he'd finally returned from the front line, nor to this awful self-imposed exile he'd enforced upon himself since Ashley's death. "Ashten, you must forgive me for arriving as I did, for storming upstairs and demanding entrance to your bedchamber, but I feared I had no other choice. Each time I've visited you these past six months, you've had Gorman turn me away, without offering any viable explanation. You haven't even agreed to see me."

"For a good reason and you shouldn't be apologizing to me. I'm the brute, not you." Sighing, he dropped his head into his open palms and speared his fingers through his silky dark locks which flowed an inch past his shoulders. He'd let his hair grow unfashionably long during his isolation, yet he looked even more desirable because of it. He appeared rakish and unkempt, yet he was also the Duke of Ashten, a man of strong will and fierce determination. She needed to ensure he returned to Society, for him to forgive himself for what had happened to Ashley and continue on with his life. Harry would want that for him too, would hate to see one of his dearest friends choosing this kind of awful isolation.

She waited as he remained quiet, naught but the crackling of the burning firewood within his fireplace filling the silence. Out his window which overlooked the manicured gardens at the rear of Blackgale House, large trees with an abundance of leafy green and yellow foliage swayed in the afternoon breeze, the sun somewhere behind the layer of gray cloud rolling in.

"I'm more than a murderer, Ellie." Whispered words as he raised his head, haunted vulnerability darkening his beautiful blue eyes. "I did whatever was necessary on the battlefield, so I wouldn't encounter the same troops on the field the next day. Lady Ashley deserved far better than me, only her adventurous nature drew me toward her right from the beginning. I could sense in her the desire for freedom, to live where nature thrived and man no longer warred. That was my desire too. London stifles me, remaining in Society even more so. I should never have attempted to pursue her, will never make that mistake with another lady again."

"Ashten, no."

"I've also allowed you to remain here for far too long." He rose and crossed to his door, opened it and bellowed, "Gorman!"

Booted footsteps pounded along the landing of the second floor and Gorman stood in the doorway, his gaze on his master, his impeccable gray jacket and trousers neatly pressed. "You called, Your Grace?"

"Please escort Lady Ellie to the door, then ensure you never permit her entrance into this house ever again, because if you do, I'll have your head for it. Am I understood?"

"Yes, understood." Gorman arched a brow at her, a flicker of camaraderie shining in his eyes, which she couldn't miss. Gorman had permitted her entrance for a reason. Yes, no more would either of them allow Ashten to wallow in his self-pity another day. Ashten's butler had been the one to care for the young duke since the day he'd turned five and lost his beloved parents in a tragic accident, and no matter Ashten's decree to have his head for any disobedience of orders, he'd truly never allow any harm to come to Gorman, not at anyone's hand, and particularly not his own. Gorman was more than his butler, and servant or not, their relationship would always stand strong.

Slowly, she stood, collected her parasol and reticule from Ashten's bed then brushed past him. Regardless of Ashten's request that she leave, she simply couldn't. Letting herself, Harry, or Gorman down this day, wasn't acceptable. Which meant it was time for her secondary plan to come into effect, because no matter what lengths she might have to go to, she'd see Ashten's heart and soul healed. She could do naught else, and thank heavens for Mr. Tidmore and the plan they'd hatched before she'd come to Ashten's doorstep to speak to him today. Winterly had introduced her to Mr. Tidmore more than a year ago, the honorable American shipping merchant now his business partner and their maritime trade ventures extremely profitable. Yesterday, after Mr. Tidmore had concluded a meeting with her brother, he'd joined her for a leisurely stroll through Mama's rose garden, just as they'd done often of late. She adored listening to his adventures on the seas, but yesterday he'd noticed her quietness and questioned her about it. Between the rose garden and a row of fastidiously trimmed topiary trees, she'd released her heartfelt burden to him about Ashten, of how Harry would detest the duke's decision to exile himself from them all.

Mr. Tidmore had agreed that the death of Lady Ashley hadn't been Ashten's fault, not at all, and that he would gladly aid her in whatever way she needed. He too wished to see the duke get back on his feet, had heard only the best things about him from Winterly. He believed Ashten had fought to keep those who lived in England safe during the fierce battles with their enemy, and he deserved to have those he'd fought for here at home, fighting for him just as fiercely in return.

It was time for the Duke of Ashten to return to the world of the living, so she and Mr. Tidmore had hatched a plan right there and then, which was why she was still here now, unable to simply walk away without fighting to see Ashten freed from these four walls.

At the door, her resolve firm and unwavering, she faced Ashten and cleared her throat. With her voice pitched low so only he could hear her, Gorman just outside the door, she murmured, "There is something I came to tell you."

"Then speak of it." He inched closer to catch her words. "Why are we whispering?"

"Because...I, ah, you should know I intend on eloping."

"Pardon?" The thin white lines either side of his mouth pinched tight. "Did I hear you right? You intend on eloping?"

"Yes, and it's all rather recent."

"Elope with whom?"

"I can't say, not when that might make my plans for a successful elopement impossible, but should foul weather take down the ship I'm soon to set sail upon, then know it has naught to do with you." She narrowed her gaze, straightened her spine, her words exactly those which she and Mr. Tidmore had agreed upon, those of a fake elopement, the added push being her decision to take to the seas, exactly as Ashley had done.

"This is unacceptable, Ellie." He grasped her arm, sent Gorman a *get lost* scowl before pulling her inside and shutting his bedchamber door with a hearty slam. "Is Winterly aware of your intended elopement?"

"No, and I have no intention of telling him either."

"You deserve a wedding day where you can celebrate your nuptials with your family and friends. Your mama will never accept such a hurried marriage." He paced from wall to wall, tugging at his cravat.

"This isn't about what Mama wants, and an elopement suits me rather well. It's what I prefer." Now she'd implemented this plan, she'd need to see it through to the end. In her discussion with Mr. Tidmore, they'd agreed that their "so called" elopement would be a ruse only, one in order to bring Ashten out of hiding, and that she'd withhold his name for as long as possible so they wouldn't need to elope in truth. Ashten's protective instincts would surely rise forth, particularly since she was Harry's sister and he'd always considered her his family too.

"Your entire family will have my head if I don't speak some sense into you right now. This elopement can't go forth." He indicated for her to return to the settee then poured another finger of liquid from the decanter into the glass he'd already drunken from.

"Might I have some of what you're drinking too?" Courage would be needed for this coming conversation. She didn't doubt that. Settling her reticule and parasol on the floor by her feet, she sat where he'd indicated.

"If you wish." He poured a splash into a second glass, handed it to her then sat in the wingchair opposite. Contemplating her with a narrowed look over the rim of his glass, he continued, "It's Scottish whisky, so drink it slowly."

"Mama says whisky is a vile brew." Although that wouldn't stop her from tasting it. She'd always had an extremely adventurous nature, a defiant one too. She lifted the glass to her lips and sipped. The potent liquid burned its way down her throat and she coughed, rather haggardly.

"I said slowly."

"How can you possibly enjoy drinking this?" Fanning her face, she cleared her throat while she eyed the harmless looking liquid, which wasn't harmless in the least.

"One garners a taste for it over time. Tell me more about your admirer."

"Betrothed, and he's incredibly dashing, enigmatic, and a man who enjoys taking chances in life." Very true. Mr. Tidmore would in fact make a rather wonderful husband if she were in fact about to elope with him. "You would never find my suitor confining himself to four walls as you have, not when the open seas and faraway lands call so deeply to him." She crossed her legs and fluffed her skirts, her trust in her ploy growing. "So, by all means, inform me if you will of all the pitfalls of an elopement to Gretna Green. Not that you've eloped yourself and have the knowledge needed to share with me."

"I have enough knowledge to know the roads between here and Gretna Green are dangerous. Highwaymen abound, and just like that"—he clicked his fingers—"your life could be snuffed out, exactly the same as Lady Ashley's was."

"I am not Lady Ashley, and my suitor would never allow any harm to come to me."

"Tell me who he is." A grating demand.

"I can give you a hint, but that's all. Hmm." She tapped her fingers on her whisky glass. To continue this ruse, she'd need to give him something to work with, so that he wouldn't think this all a ploy, and Mr. Tidmore had offered a few suggestions during their conversation, so she started with the first. "My betrothed and I danced at the ball I attended a fortnight ago."

"You've known him for only a fortnight?" Ashten gasped and shot to his feet. Swigging down the rest of his whisky, he half-walked half-limped to his window, the brunt of cannon fire he'd taken on the battlefield injuring his leg badly. "That's unacceptable. A fortnight isn't nearly long enough to know a man."

"I've known him for far longer than a mere fortnight, and Harry would tell me to follow my heart, which is what I'm doing. Please, don't give me a lecture on what I can and can't do."

"Are you in love with this chap?"

"Pardon?" She hadn't expected that question.

"You heard me. Do you love him?"

"No." A ploy this might be, but he still deserved her honesty where she could offer it. "But once we're wed, love will surely come. Already we are good friends, and holding such a deep friendship first is extremely important to me." The truth, the words rolling from her tongue with ease. She attempted another sip of whisky and this time the liquid didn't burn but instead sent a rush of warmth to her belly.

"Please, Ellie, you must reconsider your decision to elope. You and Harry are the only sane people I know in this world and I'd rather you not dispel that notion by running off and eloping." Leaning one hip against the windowsill, he knocked the rest of his drink back. "Tell me this is all a ploy and I will forgive you for the lie immediately."

"There is no ploy, and if you wish to meet the gentleman, come to the Atkinson's soiree tomorrow night. I'm expecting to see him there, then perhaps you'll be able to discover exactly who he is." Mr. Tidmore's idea. Once she'd mentioned the elopement and sparked Ashten's concern to rise, then her cohort had insisted she'd need to continue luring Ashten from these four walls by inviting him to an evening out within Society. She motioned out his window. "You would surely have received an invitation and the Atkinson's property is right next door. Your rear gardens do border their rear gardens."

"There's an invite somewhere in my mail." His blue eyes blazed with frustration as he narrowed them on her. "Although I'm not leaving Blackgale House to attend any soiree, even to discover who your 'so called' betrothed is."

"So, you intend on remaining hidden for the remainder of your life?"

"For the safety of the innocent ladies within Society, yes."

"You're a duke."

"I realize that."

"You have no heir."

"I have a remote third cousin who shall inherit my title and lands upon my death. He will do fine enough."

"Ashten, honestly." Heaving to her feet, she thrust her hands on her hips. "This is not a reasonable way to live. You must forgive yourself and cease this self-exile. If you don't wish to attend the Atkinson's gathering, then come and visit Winterly and Mama at home. Sophia and Olivia miss you dearly, and neither my sisters or I will ever saddle you to us by attempting to turn your head. You are family, will always be family."

"You have very smoothly maneuvered this conversation back around to me when it is you and your intention to elope we were discussing. Tell your suitor you've changed your mind, that you no longer wish to elope."

"I will do no such thing. I am four and twenty and must accept a proposal soon. The man I've chosen will do well enough."

"You are barely out of short skirts."

"Oh, for goodness sake." She clenched her teeth. "I left my short skirts behind six years ago. I am not a girl anymore, but a woman proper." How could he possibly still see her as a girl? Of course, she'd run around after him and Harry in her youth, particularly while they'd stayed at Winterly Manor in the country which ran adjacent to Ashten's duchy at Blackgale Park, but those days had surely come to an end when Ashten and Harry had donned their regimentals and joined the 18th Royal Hussars. Seven years ago, that had been, the year before she'd had her first Season. Shaking her head to clear her thoughts, she firmed her resolve and eyed the man before her. "I must also consider my sisters and their future. Winterly certainly won't allow Sophia to wed until I have, and Sophia is enamored with the Earl of Donnelly's youngest son, James Hargrove."

"Winterly loves you, would never force you into a marriage you didn't desire."

"As I love Sophia, and would never wish to halt her from marrying the man she wishes to wed."

"Hargrove is about to join the hussars. He'll be gone within the month."

"Pardon?" Shock coursed through her. "You must be wrong."

"Hargrove paid a call here yesterday and we spoke."

"You're accepting callers?"

"Only those of my fellow comrades, of which Hargrove is now counted amongst that number."

"Hargrove would have told Sophia if he intended on joining the hussars." She fluttered a hand over her heart and paced the floor. "Goodness. Sophia will be devastated if what you say is true."

"The viscount Major Lord Bishophale and his brother, Captain Poole, have made the call for as many able-bodied men as possible to join them when they return to the front line." He gripped his thigh, his fingers clenching deep into his injured leg. "If I hadn't suffered this dratted wound, I would join the call-to-arms too. Unfortunately, though, I'd only be an impediment during the heat of a battle."

"You'd truly return to the front line if you could?"

"Without any hesitation."

His firm answer ricocheted through her, like jagged stone tearing at her heart. For seven years, she'd feared losing both him and Harry, yet not once in all that time had Ashten written to her as Harry had done, to promise her he'd return, then when she'd learnt of Ashten's fall during a battle and subsequent injury, she'd been beside herself with worry. Only when he'd returned and recovered sufficiently enough to get out and about, he'd begun courting Lady Ashley and not her. Not once had he ever returned her feelings, which had pained her greatly, although one couldn't force another to love them and that she'd come to understand well these past six months.

Drawing in a deep breath, she collected her reticule and parasol, stood and dipped her head toward Ashten. "I apologize for having to leave, but I should speak to Sophia as soon as I can." For now, her sister must come first. "I can't withhold this kind of information from her, not when she needs to know about Hargrove's decision to join the hussars."

"No apology needed, and I'll write a letter to Harry if you wish, to ask him to watch over Sophia's suitor while they're at war. They'll be fighting together in the hussars."

"Please, I'd appreciate that." Harry wouldn't let anything happen to Hargrove, not while on his watch.

Chapter 2

Ashten stepped out of his chamber and gripped the balustrade, his hands fisted around the ornate polished railing overlooking the foyer below. Gorman had just closed the front door, Ellie now gone. His man glanced at him while his valet, Riggman, scuttled out of sight into the drawing room. Furious with his staff, he stormed downstairs and made certain to give his butler a look that conveyed his immense displeasure. "I want your word, Gorman, that you'll never allow Lady Ellie entrance again."

"Of course, Your Grace."

"Don't fail me, not once more." Aggravated, he swept past Gorman and stormed down the narrow flight of stairs leading to the basement. Cursing under his breath, he pounded on, the top of his head brushing the low ceiling and his shoulders sweeping against the sides of the musty stone passageway.

Gorman and Riggman could be as bad as each other, both having defied his orders in the past when they'd believed doing so was in his best interests. The two could also be as thick as thieves at times, but neither one of them could he ever do without. He'd been a mere five years of age when his parents had passed away in a tragic accident. They'd settled into their carriage, off for their yearly trip to Bath, all while he'd waved farewell from the front step of Blackgale Park, his country estate.

Gorman had towered over him on his right and Riggman his left, then an hour later while he'd been attending a piano lesson in the music room, the coachman had staggered back into the house, all bloodied and bruised, his arm bent at a terrible angle and grief awash on his face. Gorman and Riggman had ridden swiftly to the overturned coach.

The news had been bad, the days following all a heartbreaking blur.

A short time later, the Earl of Winterly, Harry's dear papa, had collected him and brought him to Winterly Manor which bordered his country estate. Harry's parents had been there for him following his own parents' death, had guided him as well as they could during his earlier years, and he'd been most grateful as well, what with growing up without any close relatives to care for him. During that time, he'd learnt to charge on, had attended Eton with Harry and enjoyed holidays with Harry's family, little Ellie always traipsing never too far behind them.

"Your Grace?" Gorman puffed as he followed him in a hasty rush, a flickering candle in hand. "In all truth, Lady Ellie was rather determined to speak to you and I would have had to inflict bodily harm on her to halt her in her tracks. I could never do such a thing, not when she is Harry's little sister and as close to you as any family member could be. By golly, she used to bake shortbread biscuits and bring them around in a tin to Blackgale Park, and she always made sure I received one too. Scrumptious they—"

"Enough, Gorman. You're meddling in my affairs again, trying to validate your actions." His head throbbed as he reached the dark and dusty cellar, his destination that of the trunk where he stored his war relics. He heaved the lid and rummaged within, while Gorman provided enough light for him to see by. There it was, what he was after, one of the tin boxes Ellie had delivered her scrumptious shortbread in, and damn Gorman for mentioning it when he knew he'd been heading downstairs to find that treasure himself, or perhaps more so the treasure within that shortbread tin. The gold ribbon he considered his good luck charm.

He flipped the lid of the tin up, snatched the stained and wrinkled letters from within the box, letters he'd received from his wee Ellie during his years marching against Napoleon Bonaparte. He'd read those letters a thousand times a piece, each one holding words he'd always kept close to his heart when donning his regimental uniform of royal blue, silver, and white. Not once had he ever written Ellie back though, but he'd had a good reason for not doing so at the time. Like not wishing to lead her on. She'd been seventeen when he'd left for the war and he hadn't missed her girlish fascination for him during their youth, but with her being six years younger than him, and his best friend's little sister as well, he'd taken great care to never encourage that fascination, and never would he.

Gently, reverently, he undid the gold silk ribbon holding the letters together and slipped it inside his inner jacket pocket, then replaced the lid and returned the tin to his trunk. Memories surged as he patted the ribbon in his pocket. Years ago, his Ellie, as she had a terrible tendency to do, had slipped out from under the watchful eye of her governess one day and followed him and Harry down to their favorite fishing spot beside the river. At only eight, she'd been skipping along the grassy river bank toward him with a beaming smile then made a terrible misstep and slipped. She'd toppled into the fast-flowing river and with Harry fishing just out of sight around the bend farther upstream, he'd yanked off his boots and jacket and dived in after her. No hesitation.

He'd kicked with all his might, caught up to her and gripped her tight in his arms. The fierce flow had dragged him half a mile downstream before he finally rounded a bend where the water slowed and lapped gently onto the pebbly sand. He'd powered to the foreshore and hauled them both out. Then once on firm ground again, she'd broken down and sobbed in his arms, her hair all wet and the gold silk ribbon fluttering loose. He'd plucked it from her soggy locks and pocketed it, then soothed her as well as he could with softly murmured words.

He'd completely forgotten to give that ribbon back to her, so he'd kept it, the only personal belonging of hers which he ever had, and each day when he'd dressed during the war he'd slipped her treasured ribbon inside his shirt pocket for good luck.

It had certainly brought him plenty of good luck too, until that fateful day when he'd taken his injury. That had been the only day he'd ever forgotten to ensure her ribbon was on him and close at hand. He'd left it in his uniform the night before, which Gorman had sent for laundering.

"Is that Lady Ellie's ribbon?" Gorman waited one step behind him at the base of the stone stairwell.

"Yes, and well you know it."

"You've a need for some of its good luck today?"

"Yes, and preferably with keeping the ribbon's owner far away from me." A wish he swiftly made, then thundered past the wine rack, seized a bottle of his favorite claret and marched back upstairs. Gorman followed one step behind him, just as his man always did. Even into the dark and ugly depths of the war, Gorman had been right at his back.

In his study, he sat in his sturdy chair before his oak desk and with a leaf of parchment in hand, set about writing Harry a letter. He would keep his promise to Ellie and ensure Harry was made aware of Sophia's suitor and to keep James Hargrove safe. He swigged straight from the bottle as he wrote, his thoughts and emotions slowly numbing, while Gorman waited at attention inside his study doorway.

Captain Harry Trentbury, my dearest friend with the most meddlesome little sister,

Someone currently frustrates me, a woman with golden

locks and equally glorious golden eyes, of which I need to issue a word of warning to you about. The eldest of your three younger sisters is about to elope with a gentleman she won't disclose the name of. I shall therefore endeavor to halt her, by whatever means I can, so fear not. I won't allow her to drown in deep waters, but to ensure she weds the right man when she is thinking clearly enough again.

In other news, I have it on good authority that James Hargrove is smitten with Sophia, and with that being the case, please keep a close eye on Hargrove as he intends on joining the 18th Royal Hussars and shall be stationed with you. You must ensure he remains safe, with no damage coming to his person.

Until your return, I give you my word again, as I did during my leave from you in Spain, that I shall make certain your loved ones don't cause too much strife while you are away across the channel. There is only one war you need to fight, that of our plight against Napoleon, and not that of hearth and home as well.

Please do return your ever-honorable self to London at your earliest convenience. I am beyond anxious for this blasted war to be done, and to hear of your adventurous travels while we've been apart.

As always, should you have need of me for any reason, dratted injured leg and all, send word and I shall find a way to escape Gorman with my pistol and saber in hand.

Your frustrated comrade and chum,
PLB.

With his missive penned, he dribbled hot wax and pressed his ring into the seal then handed the letter to his butler who'd moved soundlessly across the room to his desk to collect it. "Pass this to Watts and have him deliver it immediately to James Hargrove at Donnelly House with the implicit instructions that this letter is to be placed directly into Captain Harry Trentbury's hands, upon his joining the 18th. Am I understood?"

"Understood, Your Grace." His butler clipped his heels together, although he remained standing in place and not moving a blasted inch.

"What now?" With a long sigh, he leaned back in his chair and linked his hands behind his head. "Say what you need to say, and make it quick."

"I've no doubt that your father, may his soul rest in peace, would be immensely proud of you. You've fought for the 18th Royal Hussars, did your duty to our king and country, but never would he wish for you to give up your life and remain in exile behind these walls. Lady Ellie was right to come here, to try and encourage your return to Society."

"No more, William."

"Did you wish to see the invitation to the Atkinson's Ball?"

He'd tear it up once he got his hands on it. "Which pile is it in?"

"The one to your right." Three piles sat to his right, all of them several inches high. He huffed a breath, while Gorman thumbed his chin. "Or perhaps it's in one of the four piles to your left."

His dratted butler could clearly see he intended on disposing of the invitation as soon as he got his hands on it, so he snarled and gave Gorman yet another aggravated look, which his man completely ignored as he straightened the hem of his jacket.

"Your Grace, have I ever mentioned that you share a great many likenesses with your father, not only from your height and build, but with your stubborn nature as well?"

He should truly reprimand his man for speaking so rudely, only Gorman was right. He could be stubborn, well, beyond stubborn. "I barely remember him, my father that is."

"You should never have lost him as you did, or your dear mother, but I shall continue to carry out my duty to them both. Of keeping a close eye on you and ensuring you remain alive and well."

"You've never fallen short of carrying out that duty, even though there have been at least a thousand times when I've wished to throttle you for your overprotective nature."

"There are times when I fear I have in fact fallen short, but my last words to them were that I'd remain diligently at your side, no matter where that might be, and that is an oath I will hold firm to until the day I take my last breath."

"You've done a bang-up job of remaining at my side, William. Have no fear there." Gorman had attended him each and every day during the seven long years he'd be in the hussars fighting for England. His butler had walked every mile he'd walked, had been close at hand during the fighting and then at his bedside throughout his long days of recovery from that final battle which had taken him down. His butler was far more than a dedicated member of his staff. He was family. Close family.

Rising from his chair, he nodded at his man. "I need you to see to my instructions with that letter, then fetch my hat and greatcoat and have Rhodes bring the coach around. I intend on visiting my clubs and shall be out until quite late. White's first, then Boodle's." He needed to uncover all he could on how Wellington progressed at the front line, particularly since that was where Hargrove was headed, and where Harry would remain until this war was done.

"Oh my, right away, Your Grace." Gorman's eyes lit up, then he stumbled to the door, halted and cast him an anxious look over his shoulder. "Did I hear your request correctly? You wish to leave the house for White's, then Boodle's? I fear I may be hallucinating."

"Yes, you heard correctly, and try not to take your last breath while you carry out my orders. I still have a great need of you to remain close at hand." This would be his first trip out his front door since his self-exile six months ago, and all because of his wee Ellie. She'd stirred his protective desires, just as she'd likely intended to.

"I can't believe you've actually decided to venture back out into your old stomping grounds." A wide grin lit his butler's face.

"Only because it's necessary. Don't expect this to be a reoccurring trip."

It was a necessity tonight, which saw him attired with his hat atop his head and greatcoat fastened as he settled onto the padded seat of his coach a short time later. Across town, he rode, and as the sun set and the skies darkened to a starless midnight-black, a low layer of cloud concealing the moon, he finally arrived at White's.

He stepped down from his carriage and breathed deep. White's stood three stories high, a regal establishment which held a great many members of the peerage as patrons. With his cane in hand and the cold of the night biting deep into his bad leg, he nodded at the doorman on duty and limped inside.

Highly polished tables graced the main dining room, with gentlemen seated in their silk vests and tailed coats enjoying a drink and a meal. Wait staff moved about the room lit with gas lamps ensconced on the walls and corner stands. The best of British game was served within these walls and the hearty aroma of grouse, partridge, wild salmon, and smoked trout flavored the air, right along with the earthy notes of tobacco pluming from the men's pipes.

Across the far side of the dining area, the viscount Major Lord Bishophale wandered in from the billiards room with his brother, Captain Bradley Poole. The two men, comrades from his time on the front line, took a seat at a corner table. They would certainly know how all fared with Wellington.

He weaved around the tables then clapped the major and his brother on the back as he came abreast of them between their seats. He'd fought at their sides for years, had forged a bond with them that would never be broken. Blood, sweat, and tears existed between them, through both good times and bad. "It's good to see you two old chaps are home on leave."

"Ashten, by Jove, take a seat and join us for dinner." Bishophale beamed. "It's good to see you too."

"How long are you home for?"

"We've already been here for three weeks, but shall remain for another two, although that all depends on how long it takes to gather together the men we need to replenish the hussars. If it takes less, we'll be away earlier, if more, then we'll bide our time. We've been at the War Office today, but had intended on paying a call to you at Blackgale House tomorrow. Word is though, that you've turned into a complete recluse these past six months after a botched involvement with a lady who eloped with a captain out to sea. My condolences on the lady's passing."

"Word is correct, but I have learnt my lesson well, thus why I rarely get out and about."

Bishophale gestured to one of the wait staff, who promptly rushed across to the major. "My brother and I will both have the trout. Bring us a bottle of your finest white wine as well." Bishophale glanced at him. "What about you, eh, Duke?"

"The partridge," he instructed the waiter as he handed the man his greatcoat and hat. He sat with his comrades and propped his cane against the side of the table where he could reach it with ease.

The waiter returned, poured a splash into Bishophale's glass and the major swirled the liquid then sipped. With a nod, he instructed, "Well done, a superb blend. Fill the glasses and set the bottle on the table."

The waiter filled their glasses and Ashten took a hearty gulp of his wine and leaned back in his chair, his gaze on the major. "I've caught word about your call-to-arms."

"Yes, we've a great need for more men, particularly considering Napoleon's next move. Word is he's about to wed Marie Louise of Austria, the nuptials taking place very soon."

The major stroked his moustache, his gaze intent and clear worry flickering within.

"You mean the Emperor of Austria's daughter?" Ashten leaned forward, his forearms braced on the table, his own worry rising.

"Yes, Marie Louise, the emperor's eldest daughter."

"Devil take it." He slumped back, cast his gaze to Captain Bradley Poole, the man having spoken about this exact possibility several months ago, particularly once he'd learned Marie Louise now neared the age of eighteen. "All your predictions thus far have come true."

"Yes, unfortunately they have." Poole thrust a hand through his short blond hair, but didn't rumple his locks one bit. His cravat was knotted to perfection, the man a handsome rake who had a way with the ladies. He was a golden child, one the sun always seemed to shine upon. "If this union goes ahead, Ashten, then Napoleon will be marrying a member from one of Europe's leading royal houses."

"Is there a way we can halt that from happening?" Allowing Napoleon the chance to cement his relatively young French Empire wasn't permissible. Ashten tapped the tabletop as the waiter returned with their meals and set the plates down. Steam swirled from his partridge and stack of roasted potatoes and carrots.

"I'm afraid not," Poole continued once the waiter had left. "Not when we suspect Marie Louise has been ordered to agree to the marriage by her father."

"Austria has endured a series of military defeats at the hands of Napoleon and they've suffered a heavy loss of their soldiers' lives." Ashten cut into his partridge.

"True, which is why Francis the Second would have agreed to this marriage of alliance. With Napoleon about to speak vows with Marie Louise, the Corsican will surely enjoy a period of peace to come, or at least peace with Austria." Poole cut into his smoked trout.

"I agree, brother." A firm nod from Bishophale. "Although never will Napoleon be permitted to obtain peace with our great nation."

"We're a threat to Napoleon and his way of life. He'll never side with us, and we'll never side with him." Ashten swigged a mouthful of wine. "I also believe that Napoleon won't be happy until he holds power over all of Europe. France is just the beginning for him. Certainly, the revolution played right into his greedy hands."

"His greediness will one day be his downfall, and what a mighty fall it will be, a drop into the depths of hell, I imagine." Bishophale lifted his glass and in complete accord, Ashten and Poole tapped their glasses against his. No love was lost between them and their enemy, and never would be.

Setting his glass down, Ashten pressed his back into the firm support of his chair. "Russia is already becoming ruined with their defeat to Napoleon, their economy faltering due to their inability to trade with us. Has there been any change on Wellington's front?"

"No, but Wellington does hold onto the hope that the Emperor Alexander the First won't stand aside and allow his country of Russia to remain in chaos for long. The moment Alexander chooses to change his country's foreign policy and join with us again, then such a decision will stir Wellington into action. We will halt Napoleon in his endeavor to take over all of Europe, and we will do it by joining forces with Russia once more."

"Napoleon is intoxicated by his power. We must break it."

"We shall, Ashten. Have no fear there." Bishophale pulled his pipe from his pocket. "Napoleon believes he has the emperors of Austria and Russia under his control, and as we have all learnt in times of war, that kind of control isn't possible. Napoleon has only gained his rise by destroying Austria and

Russia and demanding the emperors of those two countries toe the line."

"Napoleon needs to be stripped of his power." Solemn words from Poole.

"And exiled to a rock somewhere in the middle of the ocean." Bishophale clasped his brother's shoulder and cast his gaze once more to Ashten. "I long to see that happen."

"Hear, hear," both Ashten and Poole chanted.

"Perhaps we should lighten our mood with a glass of good port. What say you both?" Bishophale lifted a hand and hailed the waiter.

"I say apple tart goes well with port." Ashten grinned at his comrades. One day they would defeat Napoleon, and that day would be hugely celebrated when it came. It was only a matter of time.

Chapter 3

The next morning, Ellie muttered and paced her bedchamber in her white linen nightgown. She'd returned from Blackgale House yesterday and spoken immediately with Sophia, who'd not long returned home herself from a carriage ride with Hargrove. James had imparted his news with her sister during their outing, that he'd be joining the 18th Royal Hussars, and Sophia had been both devastated and immensely proud of him. With her sister's acceptance of what was to be, Ellie had had no choice but to offer her own heartfelt acceptance as well. What a horrendous war though. Thousands upon thousands of good men had perished, innocent women and children too.

"Good morning, Lady Ellie." Penny, her maid, peeked around her chamber door. "Do you wish for aid in dressing?"

"Yes, come in." She shook her head of her dreadful thoughts. A new day had dawned, one she intended on embracing. Harry would expect naught less from her, and she expected the same from herself too.

In her aproned skirts, Penny bustled inside and swished open the heavy lilac drapes either side of her window overlooking the rear gardens. Dark gray clouds covered the sky, the promise of rain high. A dismal day for certain, not that she'd ever allowed London's harsh weather to keep her indoors, or from her duties which she needed to carry out, the most important still being the Duke of Ashten and her quest of aiding him.

Lifting her chin, she set her firm resolve in place. "Perhaps I'll wear something bright and cheerful today, a snub if you will at the weather."

"What a wonderful idea." Smiling, Penny poked her head inside her closet and thumbed through the gowns, before plucking one from the rail. "Might I recommend this sunshine-yellow day dress?"

"You might, and it's a wonderful recommendation. I also need you to lay out the empire evening gown which arrived from the dressmaker's yesterday for this evening's soiree at the Atkinson's home. I'll wear it with the matching burgundy slippers that came with it."

"I'll ensure your gown is steamed before I lay it out, my lady." Penny dressed her with swift efficiency and once Ellie was clothed and her leather soled slippers on, she sat in the chair before her dressing table while Penny brushed her hair and arranged her locks high on her head.

From the fanciful top knot, a fall of golden curls lay loose in places and bobbed about her shoulders. A little beeswax smeared across her lips, her cheeks rouged, and she was ready to take on this new day.

Downstairs, she trod and found Mama in the drawing room seated on the blue brocade settee, a lacy cap atop her golden hair wisped with streaks of silver, her beloved embroidery in hand. She brushed a kiss across Mama's head and settled herself in the elegant padded chair across from her. She'd always adored sitting and watching Mama stitch with such an artful hand. Mama looped the wine-colored thread through the cotton and completed the stitching of a vibrant burgundy rose within a thick bush of greenery, the rose bush identical to Mama's favorite one in her rose garden outside. "Is that piece you're stitching depicting the rose bush Papa gave you?"

34

"Yes." A soft smile lifted Mama's lips. "Your dear papa planted it himself, the very week you were born. He was eager for me to come outside and see it, so I bundled you in blankets and snuck outside with you. It was a dreary winter day, thick with fog and misty rain, and the thorny rose bush he planted was bare, but the coming spring it was awash with flowers." Mama continued stitching. "Speaking of that day. It was four and twenty years ago now."

"Yes, isn't that interesting." She barely suppressed her smile. Mama could be quite meddlesome when she wished, a trait she'd certainly picked up from her, and one she'd never complain about.

"Two children I had by your age as well."

"That is even more interesting." She wanted to giggle, gave a snort instead as she tamped it down.

"If you wished to accept one of the many proposals you keep receiving, you too could be wed and admiring your own rose bushes within your own rose gardens, mayhap with a child or two in your arms." Another stitch, one teasing brow raised. "Perhaps you might consider saying yes instead of no to your next suitor. Five there have been so far this Season, so let's not send a sixth skittering away, shall we?"

"Mama, you are so good at keeping count. I wasn't aware there'd been five already." She folded her hands in her lap, as primly as she could.

"Dearest, I have five children and not one of them has given me a grandchild yet, so you can be assured I'll continue keeping count until one of you do." Mama would too. She never handed out her threats lightly.

"I have a wonderful idea." Leaning forward, she cleared her throat. "What we need to do is find Winterly a wife." Which would keep Mama busy and her attention off her. "You and I could scour through the young ladies attending the Atkinson's ball this evening and ensure plenty of introductions are made."

"Unfortunately, Winterly isn't currently searching for a wife." Mama shoved her needle in with far less precision and muttered, "He insists he's too busy with his maritime adventures, and speaking of those adventures, Mr. Tidmore and you enjoyed a particularly long stroll in my rose garden two days ago. You two seemed to be having a rather deep and meaningful conversation. What was it all about?"

"We spoke of the piano and the pieces we're practicing together." She'd never disclose the actual truth to Mama, that they'd hatched a plan to get Ashten out of Blackgale House, one that required the ruse of an elopement.

"He's so charming." Mama adjusted her eyeglasses which ensured each small stitch was placed just right. "Even though he's an American, his mother is English and the daughter of a Baron. Were you aware?" A glance over those eyeglasses.

"He's spoken of his mother often while we've played the piano together. She taught him, his elder brother, and three younger sisters how to play." She rose and crossed to her treasured piano under the window then trailed one finger along the polished golden-red wood surface.

"Do you favor him at all?" Another pointed question.

"In what way do you mean?"

"I'm asking if you intend on allowing the gentleman to get down on one knee at any point in the future?"

"To do what exactly? Inspect my slippers?" She probably shouldn't torment Mama so.

"You are a terrible tease, Ellie Marie, and so very like your papa in that regard." A shake of her finger, a smile evident in her eyes. "I do miss his quick wit and ability to lighten any mood."

"You wouldn't mind ever so much if you only saw me half the year? Mr. Tidmore travels a great deal." She collected the piano music she'd played the night before from the stand and tucked it away in the top drawer of the side table.

"I would miss you dreadfully should you travel, but every

mother must allow her children the chance to spread their wings and soar from the nest. That is the way of life."

"Mr. Tidmore is both caring, considerate, and honorable." She'd noted that about him from the very beginning.

"Yes, he's a most honorable gentleman, and he and Winterly get along so incredibly well."

"Good morning, Mama, Ellie." Sophia breezed in wearing a vivid blue morning gown with fluttering ribbons tied under the high waist. "Winterly and who get along well, if I might ask?"

"Mr. Tidmore of course." Mama beamed at Sophia. "You look delightful in that color, my dear. It's like that of a clear summer sky."

"James Hargrove adores this color on me too. We're to enjoy a carriage ride together later this afternoon." Blushing, Sophia popped a kiss on Mama's cheek, settled beside her on the settee and folded her hands in her lap. "I've just been with Olivia and she isn't feeling well, an ache of the belly she said."

"Yes, I've already taken her some chamomile in her tea earlier this morning." Mama set her embroidery aside in the cane basket at her feet, their snoozing puppy in its padded basket on her other side. "If she rests adequately, then hopefully she'll still be able to join us at the Atkinson's ball this evening. Winterly is certainly looking forward to escorting all of his sisters to the gathering."

"James will be attending the ball too." Sophia's gaze softened, her eyes watering a touch.

"All will be well, dearest." Gently, Mama rested her arm around Sophia's shoulders and hugged her to her side. "This war won't keep your beau away for long, and he'll be serving with the 18th Royal Hussars, right alongside Harry. Such an honorable young man Hargrove is."

Ellie detested seeing her sister in such pain, and no matter Sophia's brave face yesterday after her sister had relayed her news about her beau, she was most definitely in pain. She hugged her sister too, then rang the bell on the side table, which caused their wee puppy to lift its head for a moment before dropping it back down again. Tea and refreshments were needed, a suitable diversion which might help turn her sister's thoughts from her current worry over Hargrove. Beast would help with that distraction too. She picked their puppy up from his cushioned basket, his floppy ears falling forward, then snuggled him in Sophia's lap. As the housemaid arrived, she asked, "Meg, please bring us some tea and scones, and don't spare the jam and cream. We need something sweet to lift our current mood."

"Right away, my lady." The maid dipped her head and disappeared out the door.

"Speaking of the hussars." Mama gently petted Beast between his ears. "I do worry about Ashten and the terrible rumors circulating about him amongst the *ton*. I miss that dear boy and wish he'd return to Society." Mama pulled her white lace handkerchief from her gown pocket and dabbed her eyes, her gaze misting. "He and Harry were always thick as thieves in their youth, and the gossip surrounding Ashten at present is awful. Why, there is no way he had anything to do with Lady Ashley's elopement and subsequent death."

"Of course, he had nothing to do with it." She wished she could tell Mama about her visit to Blackgale House, but unfortunately ladies never called upon an unwed gentleman unless they had some form of actual business to discuss, and her business of drawing the duke out of his self-exile, wouldn't be a sufficient enough excuse for Mama. No, only her sisters truly understood her need to go. It was also best she moved this conversation along too. She didn't wish to make a mistake and mention something about Ashten by chance.

"Here we are, my ladies." The maid returned and set the tea tray on the table.

"I'll serve, Meg." Doing so would keep her hands busy. She poured the tea, handed Mama and Sophia their cups and perched on the settee next to her sister as she sipped the hot brew sweetened with honey. She munched on a scone smeared in jam and topped with a mound of cream that wobbled precariously since it sat so high. Delicious. Only when she eyed the last remaining scone, Mama gave her a disapproving frown.

"One scone eases one's hunger, Ellie Marie, and two is simply giving into gluttony." Mama promptly pinched the last scone and sat back with her treasure, a gleeful smile on her lips.

Sophia laughed and slipped the last bite of her scone between her lips. "We clearly get our sweet tooth from you, Mama."

"I'm sure you do." Mama reached across and patted Ellie's hand. "This evening at the Atkinson's, I shall be introducing you to Lady Foxeworth's son who arrived into town recently from their country estate. Lady Foxeworth paid me a visit yesterday while you and Sophia were both out."

"Oh, I'm sorry I missed her."

"You were out for an inordinately long length of time." Suspicion clouded Mama's eyes. "Did you have trouble in town?"

"Yes, I, ah, got distracted at Madam Gonnier's shop and spent far too much time there." She set her cup and saucer down, plucked Beast from Sophia's lap and cuddled him close to her chest. To her sister, she said, "I have my gown for the Atkinson's soiree, but I'd hoped to visit Mrs. Smithmore's shop and peruse her hats, ribbons, and wraps. Would you like to come with me? The milliner mentioned a new French organdie which had arrived, and I haven't yet had a chance to see it."

"Of course, I'll come. I'm in need of a mask for the Campton's War Society Charity Ball and I've yet to find one that suits my costume." Sophia stood and eyed Mama. "Would you like to join us, Mama?"

"No, you two have a lovely day out together. I wish to remain here in case Olivia needs me. I'll shop for a mask tomorrow, particularly since Winterly and Olivia still require masks too. There's still plenty of time."

"Should I see any masks you might like, I'll ask Mrs. Smithmore to set them aside." Sophia swished out the door, calling over her shoulder to Ellie, "I'll just fetch my cloak and meet you in the foyer."

"I'll be right with you." She kissed Mama's cheek, handed her Beast, then dashed out the door after Sophia.

With her own cloak fastened, she stepped into the coach after her sister and following the short trip into town, wandered into the milliner's shop. While Mrs. Smithmore spoke at the front counter with another customer about hats, she and Sophia stood at the back sifting through the filmy fichus of pale pastel colors.

"I have to admit, I too have considered sneaking by Blackgale House for a visit." Sophia kept her voice low as she made that admission. "Is Ashten well, other than for his injured leg?"

"He appeared well, except for his atrocious mood. It was as black as I've ever seen it."

"What he needs is a good dose of *Harry*." Her sister draped a pearl-colored silk wrap over her shoulders and eyed her reflection in the oval standing mirror. "It's been an age since Ashten last visited our home and enjoyed an evening with us. I miss him."

"He simply won't forgive himself for what happened to Lady Ashley."

"Well, now you've forged ahead with your plan of a fake elopement to draw him out, my fingers are crossed that Ashten will take the bait and attend tonight's soiree." The bell over the door rang and another lady entered the shop and drew closer toward them. Sophia caught her hand and led her farther down the aisle toward the ribbon display. Once alone again, her sister continued, "Mr. Tidmore is so wonderful to have come on side with you. Do you like him, Mr. Tidmore that is?"

"I do. He's so easy to like, but I can't be seen alone with him tonight, but rather dancing with a number of eligible men who would all make suitable beaux."

"Yes, because if word gets out that you're about to elope, whether that is a ruse or not, you don't need for that to become an actuality, unless of course you wish to elope with the delectable Mr. Tidmore."

"You think he's delectable?"

A smile from her sister.

Chapter 4

That evening, the long burgundy skirts of her empire evening gown swishing about her ankles, Ellie stood at the fringes of the Atkinson's ballroom and cooled herself with her delicate white-feathered fan. Sophia danced with James Hargrove, her sister's cheeks all aglow, just as they'd been when Sophia had returned from her afternoon carriage ride through the park with James. Sophia had chosen to embrace every possible moment she could with her suitor before he rode out with the hussars into battle.

"You appear a million miles away." Olivia nudged her arm as the music and chatter from the crowd drifted over them.

"Sophia and James are on my mind." She wished only for her loved ones to experience happiness.

"They're on my mind too." Her sister tucked a golden lock behind her ear as she snuck a look through the dancing couples on the floor and found Sophia and Hargrove. A soft sigh escaped her lips. "She's so in love. It's impossible to miss."

"When I spoke to Ashten, he promised to write to Harry and ensure he watched over Hargrove when he joined him."

"Harry will keep him safe. That is a certainty." Olivia swayed gently to the music, her white slippered toes peeking out from under the voluminous folds of her pink skirts. Her sister had recovered from her illness and appeared in her usual good spirits, her cheeks rosy and glowing.

"Is there any particular gentleman you'd like to dance with tonight?"

"That would be telling." A cheeky smile from Olivia. "What of your dance card?"

"I've left a few dances free."

"In case a dashing hussar changes his mind and takes you up on your offer to join us tonight?" Olivia lifted Ellie's card which dangled from her wrist with a dainty white ribbon and perused it. "Perhaps I should write the duke's name on this card for him. I don't know how he could possibly turn down a request to join you after your visit."

"He'll turn it down if that's what he wants to do. He can be as obstinate as Harry when he wishes."

"Well, if any of us had the chance to draw Ashten out of his self-exile, it would be you." Her sister glanced across at the refreshment table, where Mama conversed with Lady Foxeworth. "Those two have had their heads bent together for half an hour. That mightn't bode well for you, dear sister."

"Mama wishes to introduce me to the lady's son, although he hasn't yet arrived by the looks."

"Good evening, ladies." Baron Herbarth whisked in and picked up Olivia's dance card and signed his name on both the next dance and the last.

Olivia gasped, her voice pitched a little too high as she said, "My lord, you can't possibly think to reserve two dances with me tonight."

"I can and now have." The baron arched a challenging brow at her sister. "Do you care to raise an argument over it?"

"I will if you try to claim both."

Hmm, what on earth had raised her sister's ire with the baron, and was something going on between the two of them that she wasn't aware of?

"I overheard a gentleman speaking"—the baron

straightened his cufflinks, a depth to his voice that brooked no argument—"about commandeering your card for himself for the remainder of the evening, so I thought it best I get in first. You can't fault me for that."

"I'm certain you heard no such thing."

"I would never speak a mistruth to a lady." With a suddenly mischievous grin lifting his lips, he went to sign a third spot, only Olivia pulled her card from his reach.

"Kind sir." Olivia fluttered her lashes. "Two dances shall be quite sufficient for you tonight, unless of course you wish to cause a stir this evening?"

Ellie couldn't help but smile at her sister's quick response and clever wit with the amorous baron. This was only Olivia's second Season, but she was already quite adept at managing herself.

"Causing quite a stir with you sounds divine." Herbarth placed one hand behind his back and bowed as he offered Olivia his arm. "Shall we begin by dancing the next set together?"

"Provided you don't give my mama anything to caution me over later, then yes."

"I shall do my best." He chuckled, and Olivia accepted the baron's arm, sent her a quick *I'm sorry* look over her shoulder and moved away into the swirling mass of dancers. Something was most certainly up between Olivia and Baron Herbarth, and she intended to discover exactly what it was, or at least she would once she'd dealt with the very frustrating Duke of Ashten. One problem at a time.

"Your sisters are like two rare butterflies fluttering about the garden tonight." Winterly stepped in beside her, the ice she'd requested of him now in his hand, his overly indulgent gaze on Sophia and Olivia as they twirled about.

"What of me? Am I not a rare butterfly too?"

"Are you seeking more compliments, dear sister?" He handed her the ice.

"I wouldn't mind one, perhaps even two if you're feeling a little generous."

With a chuckle, he tapped her nose. "You aren't a rare butterfly, but instead a ray of sunshine brightening the entire garden bed."

"I am?" Her brother appeared to be in a good mood tonight.

"Yes, which is what Mr. Tidmore told me this afternoon during one of our meetings, and which I'm simply repeating." A twinkle lit his eyes, the blue the exact same shade as Papa's had been. No matter five years had now passed since Papa's death, she'd still never forget anything about him. Her brother held the same dark hair as Papa had, as well as cut short and combed back, all except for one errant lock that curled forward over his brow.

"I love you," she whispered to him, unable to help herself.

"I love you too." He grinned and said, "I noticed you and Mr. Tidmore had quite the deep conversation in the garden the other day."

"You and Mama were clearly both watching me."

"Did Mama speak about it?"

"Yes, and I've been told she heartily approves of him." She sipped her cool drink. "Do you?"

"Absolutely."

"So, if Sophia and Olivia are rare butterflies, and I'm like a ray of sunshine brightening the entire garden bed, then what kind of spring flower would you like for yourself, dear brother? A fragrant rose, or perhaps an elegant lily?"

"You're turning this conversation back on me."

"Yes, so answer the question."

"Well." He twiddled with the buttons of his blue silk waistcoat, his gaze deep and suddenly filled with longing. "In truth, I'd rather have a wildflower, one which bloomed with freedom no matter where it was planted." He eyed her circumspectly. "Ever since your first Season, you've never truly allowed any man to get too close to you, yet with Mr. Tidmore you seem more at ease. You two also have a great deal in common, not only with your love for family, but in how quick your minds both are. My question therefore, is if he comes to me requesting a betrothal, I would like your approval in considering it. There is Sophia and Olivia to think of. You can't continue turning down every eligible gentleman who offers for you."

"I understand." Except the only man she'd ever truly wished to wed had decided on his return from the war to pursue another woman. "I shall let you know in due course."

"Thank you, but why is it I can still sense something is wrong. Is your heart stuck on a certain man you used to follow around our country estate as a child?"

"Which man would that be?"

"We've always been honest with each other, Ellie, and I'm certain you're aware of whom I'm speaking of. You certainly have too much love to give to ever be content as a spinster." Winterly motioned to the balcony door. "Take a look outside. That is the man I speak of."

Frowning, she did as he'd requested. Beyond the rear garden wall, candlelight shone from the upper floor of Blackgale House, and six windows across from the left, within the chamber belonging to the Duke of Ashten, the outline of one very familiar man took form. A man with a telescope currently raised to his eye."

"The duke seems rather intent on keeping you in his sight tonight."

"The coward and cheat." She muttered the words under her breath. Good grief. She should have considered that Ashten might find another way to discover who her suitor might be, rather than by leaving his house to attend this ball. Hackles raised, she smiled sweetly at her brother. "I believe the duke is simply viewing the merriment taking place here tonight. You surely haven't forgotten how he chose to woo Lady Ashley rather than me on his return from the war?"

"True, although I doubt he ever would have actually gone through with asking for Lady Ashley's hand, not when you kept drawing his attention." He settled one hand on her shoulder, his palm warm and his touch comforting, just as it always was. "Hear me out, if you will, Ellie."

"Of course."

"My belief," he murmured, keeping his words between the two of them, "is that Ashten would have eventually come to his senses and paid a call on you."

Her brother had to be delusional. "Winterly, Ashten has never once asked me to dance with him, not even when he had leave from the hussars and socialized, nor has he ever requested a stroll through the gardens, or a ride in the park, or any other such activity one might embark on while paying those calls. He has expressed no interest in me whatsoever." Not in all the years she'd known him. Even yesterday, when they'd been alone together in his bedchamber, he'd stated he had no desire for Winterly to catch her there, that he had no wish for any union between them.

"We shall see who is right or wrong then, shall we?" A teasing gleam lit her brother's eyes.

"You are impossible sometimes."

"Yes, but one way or another, I will see you wed before the end of this year is upon us. That is the next mission I've assigned myself."

Wonderful, she'd now become her brother's next mission. Not surprising though, and at least he wouldn't marry her off to someone who didn't appeal to her. He loved her too much to do so.

As a passing waiter came abreast of them and extended his tray, she set her empty glass on it.

Across the room, two late arrivals strode in, Major Lord Bishophale and his brother, Captain Bradley Poole, the two men good comrades of Harry's. They usually fought alongside each other in the hussars, the two men now currently at home on leave as they sought to ensure a fruitful call-to-arms. She'd even danced with Captain Poole at Almack's a fortnight ago, the minuet, and never had she had such a spirited dance partner as the captain.

Winterly cast his gaze on the major and captain. "There are two men I wish to speak with."

"As do I."

"That sounded promising." A chuckle from her brother. "Bat your lashes, dear sister."

"I didn't mean speaking with them in that sense. Really!" she huffed. "You are beyond impossible sometimes, and Mama always tells me to watch my tongue, not bat my lashes. You should do the same."

"A sound idea. Then bat your lashes and watch your tongue." Still chuckling, Winterly escorted her across the room, directly to the two men he wished to speak with. "Good evening, gentlemen. Lady Ellie and I were hoping to enquire about your health. My sister is always worried about our men who serve. Is all well with you both?"

She sent Poole an adoring smile, batting her lashes high and wide. "Yes, I'm always rather concerned with the health and wellbeing of our officers. I greatly admire all you do in serving our country."

"That service is a delight to offer." Poole extended his hand to her, his head dipped and gaze steadfast on hers. "All is most certainly well with my brother and I. Have no fear there."

"How much longer are you on leave?" She placed her fingers in his and he kissed her knuckles.

"Two weeks, possibly three. With the call-to-arms we've raised, all is going well."

"I'm aware James Hargrove will be joining you."

"Yes, a good man he is." As the opening chords of a minuet

rang out, Poole arched a brow at her. "Might I ask if you're free for the next dance?"

"As it happens, I am free." She smiled sweetly at her brother standing next to the major. "Will you be all right on your own?"

Winterly laughed and shook his head. "You are entertaining."

"Stay out of trouble while I'm gone." She pecked her brother on the cheek then linked her hand through Poole's offered arm.

The captain, his gaze bright and his smile infectious, swept her onto the dancefloor amongst the couples in his fine cream silk pantaloons and tan tailed coat adorned with ruffles and sashes. "You look absolutely delightful tonight, Lady Ellie."

"Please, call me Ellie. This is our second minuet, which calls for a great deal of gazing into each other's eyes, and as such demands the use of first names."

"Then you must call me Bradley, and I agree, this dance does call for a great deal of gazing into each other's eyes."

"I'm almost certain the minuet is truly the cause of many a young lady falling under her dance partner's spell while the aforementioned gazing is underway." She pointed her right toe and slowly sank down on her left leg in the most elegant curtsy she'd ever performed, while across from her the captain bowed deeply, the buckles on his black shoes shining bright. Once again, and so very quickly, he'd sparked her competitive spirit, just as he'd done during their first minuet. "Are you competitive at all, Bradley?"

"Exceptionally competitive, and I'm well trained in this dance. Let us see who can break whose gaze first?"

"Oh, I do love a good challenge." Excitement swirled inside her as they both joined into a set of eight with three other couples. As the music began proper, she and the other ladies moved into the center, slow and graceful in their step, then they joined hands together. To the right, they circled as their partners circled in the opposite direction. Gliding, as gracefully as she could, she broke the circle to join with Bradley, just as the other ladies did with their partners. They circled each other, fingers touching ever so softly, gazes on each other's. "Point your toe out a little farther." She couldn't contain her smile as she offered the advice to her partner.

"My toes are pointed perfectly, my lady." Poole raised a curious brow. "Are you trying to make me miss a step?"

"I would never do any such thing." She bit her lip in an attempt to stifle her giggle, just managed to do so as well.

"I'm certain you are." His lips lifted as he moved around her, never allowing her to get too far from him and always with his gaze on hers. "No wonder your brother called you entertaining."

"That part is true. I am forever amusing him." The dance separated them as she moved around another gentleman beside her, a brief contact, then moving in division, aligning with another lady, then back again to Bradley.

"I prefer a lady with spirit, and yours is rather commendable." He swept a hand around her back and led her in a circle, his blue eyes twinkling with merriment. "If I may ask, do you ride as well as you dance?"

"I learnt to ride before I could walk." Papa had been her teacher, his skill atop a horse unparalleled to any another, well, except for Ashten. The duke had overtaken her father's ability by his eighteenth year, and she'd witnessed his progression with wonder. While at their country home which bordered Blackgale Park, she often caught sight of Ashten flying across the meadows atop his sleek black stallion. He was well known as a breeder of some of the finest horseflesh in the country.

"Then I would be greatly honored if you would consider a ride with me about the park, perhaps on the next fine day?"

"I would adore that." She truly would, and to continue with

her plan, she needed to be seen with as many different gentlemen as she could in order to keep Ashten guessing about who her intended might be, particularly since the man in question still stood in shadow at his window observing her.

After the minuet ended, a country set began and she accepted the hand of yet another gentleman who'd marked her dance card upon her arrival at the ball. Throughout the evening, she danced with one eligible gentleman after another, her gaze slipping toward Blackgale House at every possible opportunity, and as unobtrusively as she could.

Chapter 5

Inside his darkened bedchamber lit only by the moon, Ashten fisted his hands and gritted his teeth as music drifted through his partially open window from the Atkinson's ballroom. He'd spent an hour watching and fuming as Ellie had danced with one young buck after another, but as yet he hadn't noticed her favoring any single gentleman over another, other than for perhaps Captain Poole. The two had taken the minuet into a challenge of sorts, of who could outstare the other. He also hadn't missed Poole splaying his hand over the small of Ellie's back for far longer than the dance required. How aggravating.

He tossed his cavalry telescope on his bed, his mind churning over their last conversation.

This is not a reasonable way to live. You must forgive yourself and cease this self-exile. If you don't wish to attend the Atkinson's gathering, then come and visit Winterly and Mama at home. Sophia and Olivia miss you dearly, and neither my sisters or I will ever saddle you to us by attempting to turn your head. You are family, will always be family.

He had no intention of giving up his self-exile, no matter he'd enjoyed leaving the house last night to return to his club, and was that the captain making another beeline for Ellie? Damn it. It was. Poole had clearly requested another dance with her, and Ellie now curtsied and nodded her agreement. He wanted to throttle them both.

Particularly Ellie, and he would, the very next time he saw her.

Which would hopefully be never.

Gah, just one little taste of being back in her company yesterday had skewered all his good intentions and somehow sent him slumping even deeper into despair. He should be purging his memories of her, not instilling new ones within his mind.

Frustration and anger brewed deeply within him too.

Bitter regret as well.

He scooped up a glass of whisky from his side table and glugged the shot down before pacing the area in front of his window, his gaze trained on one extremely annoying woman who was looking so adoringly into the eyes of a damn fine officer, a friend, and a man he'd always held in great esteem.

Could Poole be the gentleman she intended on eloping with?

Poole had only been back in town for three weeks, so it was a distinct possibility, and it wasn't as if he didn't already know Ellie. The two socialized in the same circles, just as he had done with her whenever he'd returned home from leave, and before he'd decided to shun Society.

Ellie had mentioned that her beau would soon be setting sail too, which could be a possibly if she intended on boarding the navy ship Poole would soon set sail upon to cross the channel. It certainly wasn't unusual for a few of the men's wives to join their husbands near the front line. Those women usually offered their aid as nurses or caregivers for the wounded and blast Ellie's charitable soul, but she wouldn't hesitate to nurse the wounded if called to do so. Not that he would ever have allowed her to follow him into battle if she'd been his wife. Not that he would ever have taken her to wife. Poole shouldn't either. Hell and damnation. He couldn't halt her from marrying Poole if her heart was truly set on the man. He growled under his breath, his fury rising.

"Your Grace?" A soft tread of footsteps halted behind him.

"Don't say a word," he clipped as Gorman waited silently and Ellie, her burgundy skirts flaring as she moved through the intricate steps of yet another dance alongside Poole, scalded his insides with her behavior, as if he'd drunken an entire bottle of whisky rather than a single shot. She twirled and for a mere moment her gaze seemed to connect with his through the open balcony doors, her long eyelashes sweeping down then back up again to expose those smoldering golden eyes of hers.

He swore viciously again. If he could, he'd be over there in a flash, tearing her away from Poole and whisking her around the dancefloor himself.

His heart clenched and shoulders slumped.

No, he wouldn't.

To date, not once had he ever held her in his arms and danced with her, not even when she'd come of age. When she'd been seventeen, he'd ridden off to war, and over the seven years since he'd joined the hussars, he'd traveled immensely, most of the time trying to blot out all thought of her.

He gave the window his back, perched his backside on the sill and glared at his butler. "I can't take the chance of hurting another innocent lady."

"Lady Ashley chose her own path."

"She sensed my desire to offer for her."

"Yet you hadn't done so when you could have."

"I was getting around to it." Gorman had been there that morning he'd intended on calling around to Lady Ashley's home so he could speak with her father, only he'd been unable to step outside his front door. For some reason, he'd gotten all flustered, which was so very unlike him.

"I've never spoken of this, Your Grace, but during your recovery from the cannon fire, there were several nights when you awoke from terrible nightmares as I tended you." His butler clasped his hands firmly behind his back. "Each time when you awoke, it was after calling Lady Ellie's name."

"She's Harry's little sister."

"She's hardly his little sister anymore." Gorman stared out the window and frowned. "She's also about to take a stroll outside with her dance partner."

"Would that still be Captain Bradley Poole?" He had no intention of turning around and laying his gaze on her again. Only danger lay down that path, as it already had this evening.

"Yes."

"What are they doing now?" Jaw clenched, he stayed his position. His butler had his uses and being observant was one of them. "Give me an exact description."

"They're standing on the balcony in full view of those inside." Gorman's frown deepened. "Although they do appear to be in a rather deep discussion, their heads bent close together."

"Tell me when they return inside." He waited, counting a full five minutes before he got impatient and growled, "Are they still conversing?"

"They are, although they're now moving deeper into the shadows, nearer the steps leading down into the garden."

"Does she have an escort?"

"No, Your Grace." Gorman snagged the telescope from the bed, extended the barrel and peered through the lens as he himself had done throughout the night. "Ah, there we are. I didn't see her sisters farther along the terrace. The captain is dropping a kiss on her gloved hand and…now returning indoors. She is with Sophia and Olivia."

"Where the hell is Winterly?" He knocked another shot of whisky down while Gorman remained on duty at the window. "Give me another update."

"All three ladies have now disappeared into the garden, with their arms linked."

"Don't take your gaze off them." Harry's sisters could cause immense trouble when left alone, and he knew that well since he'd all but grown up with them. With his tension doubling, he gritted his teeth. "Blast it, William. What is Winterly thinking letting them wander about the gardens all alone?"

"Gads." Gorman dropped the telescope with a *thump* on the mat underfoot. "Lady Sophia and Lady Olivia are returning to the ballroom."

"They've left Ellie alone?" He bounded in front of the window and searched the darkened gardens. "Where is she?"

"At our rear gate."

It clicked shut and Ellie whisked down his garden path in the moonlight. She was a vision in her gown of burgundy chiffon, the empire neckline cut low and the dainty capped sleeves barely holding onto her shoulders.

"Ashten?" She halted underneath his window, her voice drifting through the three-inch opening at the bottom.

Fingers digging into the sill, he stayed his position.

"Lady Ellie is now attempting to get your attention." Gorman handed him the telescope.

"So I noticed." He pushed away from the sill and set the telescope on the side table next to his whisky glass.

"Good evening, Gorman. I see the duke is with you, but not answering me."

"A good evening to you too, my lady." Gorman lifted a hand and waved to the imp. "Have you been enjoying yourself at the ball?"

"Most certainly. Would you be so kind as to ask the Duke of Ashten to meet me by his fishpond?"

"Of course. I shall do so immediately."

"I'm not meeting you by my fishpond!" He thrust his window fully open, the lip hitting the top catch, and his blasted enchanting imp smiled even wider.

"I wished to dance with you, or do you think I'm being too forward in asking?"

"You're being far too forward."

"I had an interesting conversation with Captain Poole tonight."

"So I noticed."

"He's asked me to go riding with him in the park on the next fine day."

"Is he your intended then?"

"I hope that next fine day is tomorrow." She twirled around, her hands in her flaring skirts and an eager smile lifting her lips.

"I asked if he's your intended?"

"You are being very forthright." She gave him a fierce frown, her smile dying away.

"You are being very devious."

"I do not have a devious bone in my body." She rubbed her arms, the wind cool as it blew inside.

"You are riddled with devious bones, and where is your wrap?"

"I left it behind." Fire glinted in her golden eyes, a fire he'd seen often over the years. She wasn't going to leave without seeing him again. He knew it to the depths of his soul.

"Leave now, Ellie, and never return." He could be just as stubborn and devious as she could be.

"The fishpond," she stated firmly again, then marched back along the path before sneaking into the bushes and disappearing behind the tree bordering his fishpond.

How incredibly frustrating.

Chapter 6

Heartbeat thumping vigorously, Ellie rubbed her chilled arms as she walked alongside the garden wall next to the shimmering waters of Blackgale House's fishpond. The sheer chiffon of her gown rustled as she trod across the grass growing damp with the coming dew of the night, while from the Atkinson's ballroom so close, the melodious notes of the next dance floated toward her.

"I told you to leave, Ellie, and to never return." Ashten, his cane in hand and limp more pronounced tonight, stomped past a tall cultivated hedge, his black cravat knotted at his neck over a black linen shirt, his black silk waistcoat buttoned. He appeared a very dominating force, only she had no intention of cowering to him. Not tonight. Not ever.

"I asked you for a dance, Your Grace."

"And I declined." He removed his superfine jacket and held it by the shoulders for her to slip her arms into, his cane resting against his hip as he did. "You're shivering."

"I'll be fine."

"Put my jacket on. I can't allow you to catch a chill while on my property." He flapped his jacket over her head and caught her within the circle of his arms, his body emitting a delicious heat that poured into her.

"I don't need your jacket." She pressed against his chest to insert some space, only he moved not an inch.

"Yes, you do." He draped it over her shoulders, his lips near her ear as he lowered his growly voice to a soft murmur, "I apologize if I seem overly grouchy tonight."

"You're always grouchy, or at least you are of late." She pushed her arms through the sleeves, his jacket completely engulfing her and his wonderfully warm scent as well.

"I apologize for saying you are riddled with devious bones."

"Why have you been lying to me?" She stared him straight in the eye.

"About what exactly?"

"You were at White's last night. Bradley informed me so himself."

"You're on first name terms with Captain Poole?"

"Did you, or did you not, leave your home and attend your club last night?"

"I did, but thankfully there are no ladies permitted at White's, which meant any innocent ladies remained safe." His gaze narrowed. "Who did you dance with a fortnight ago?"

"Not you." She inched forward a step, until her slippered toes touched his booted Hessians. "You also need to worry less about me and more about yourself."

"What I worry about is this dratted war."

"You've clearly uncovered something of interest at White's. What was it?" She was eager to hear more about this awful war and whenever possible, did so.

"I spoke to Poole and Bishophale while at White's. There's great worry over Napoleon's next move. Word is he's about to wed Marie Louise of Austria, the Emperor of Austria's daughter."

"Oh dear." Her heart sank. Not good news at all. She rested her hands on Ashten's shirtfront. "If Napoleon is given the chance to cement his relatively young French Empire, then he will attempt to take England next. He'll think nothing of it."

"I agree, which means the war could be about to escalate, and far beyond what it already has."

"This is dreadful news." Agitated, she stepped back and followed the gravel path past a pink flowering bush toward the gazebo in the corner. The gazebo stood supremely elegant, painted a splendid white with ivy climbing one side and a white rose bush the other. She grasped her skirts and walked up the two steps then eased down onto the bench rimming the side. She rearranged her skirts and tugged the sides of Ashten's jacket more firmly at the front. "What of Wellington?"

"Wellington continues to hold onto the hope that Emperor Alexander the First won't stand aside and allow Russia to remain in chaos. The moment Alexander chooses to change his country's foreign policy and join with us again, Wellington will be there to stand beside him and ensure Napoleon is halted in his endeavors to take over all of Europe." Ashten sat on the bench next to her, tucked his cane under the bench and wrapped one arm around her shoulders. "Are you still cold?"

"Less so now." Goodness, she feared for Harry. "This all means more warring and an inevitable loss of life. Harry will fight to the death to ensure our protection, that those of us here in England remain safe and well."

"All our men will fight, and they won't stop until Napoleon surrenders and this war is done." He dropped a kiss on the top of her head. "You're shaking."

"Because I need to tell you something of a personal nature, and I need for you to listen to me."

"I'd rather you didn't have any need to speak to me at all." He removed his arm from her shoulders and frowned at his hands. "I do apologize. I didn't mean to overstep any boundaries between us, only the more I'm around you, the more I forget myself."

"You can forget yourself around me as often as you please."

"That sounded rather brazen, Ellie."

"Maybe it's time for a little brazen between us."

"I have no need for a wife." He shook his head. "We had this conversation during your last visit."

"Yes, and I'm well aware you've no desire for that wife to be me." She tried to give him her most condescending look, only she likely failed since he arched his brow in that way he did when he saw right through her.

"I've taken mistresses in the past," he blurted, "and they satisfy any demands I have quite nicely."

"Ashten!" Heat flared in her cheeks, and although she should remain quiet, she also couldn't help but appreciate Ashten's current honesty with her. "What I mean is, ah, are all men who don't wish to take a wife inclined to feel that way? That they could simply take a mistress to satisfy their body's demands?"

"No, not all men feel that way." His gaze narrowed, the piercing blue darkening to a midnight shade.

"I've kissed only two men," she blurted this time.

"Who? Wait." He held up a hand. "No, don't tell me."

"I would have only kissed one man, other than for the fact that I needed to know if the first man was any good at kissing, so I kissed the second man to be sure."

"And your decision on those kisses?"

"I truly didn't care for either of them. I thought kissing would be more enchanting, or at least leaving me with the desire for more than a single kiss, to wish for a second or a third with the same gentleman."

"They obviously kissed you respectfully."

"There are two ways to kiss someone?"

"Yes, there certainly are."

"How intriguing, although I can hardly ask a man to kiss me, ah, without respect, so I might learn the difference."

"How does Winterly deal with you?" He shook his head

61

and blew out a long breath.

"With great entertainment." She couldn't help her giggle.

"Let me show you what a disrespectful kiss is then." He held out his hand then arched a brow. "Put your hand in mine, and I'll take that as a yes of your acceptance."

"You'll truly kiss me? Disrespectfully?" She'd always wished for such a moment as this, and since this might be the only opportunity she ever had, she placed her gloved hand in his and showed her ready acceptance with her actions.

"You are far too trusting."

"You would never hurt me."

"Let's hope not." Gently, he turned her hand over and finger by finger, tugged on the soft silk until he'd removed her glove then done, dropped it onto the bench beside him and brought her palm to his mouth. With one warm and incredibly soft kiss against her skin, the midnight blue of his eyes twinkling bright, he asked, "Are you ready?"

"Is there anything I need to do during this disrespectful kiss?"

"No, not a thing." As the opening notes of a waltz floated toward them, he rose and drew her to her feet, then slowly, carefully, he pulled her into his arms.

"I can't believe we're about to dance."

"And kiss."

"Yes, that too." She placed her gloved hand on his shoulder, her ungloved hand still held firm in his. Never had she ever danced this close to a gentleman before. Six inches was the required etiquette, and there was less than three inches between them right now. "You look dashing, as if you've dressed for this ball tonight, then chose to remain indoors."

"Since we're being honest, I was extremely tempted to come." He swept her around the inner circle of his gazebo, his hand firm on her waist and his limp barely noticeable. "Did you have to dance"—he cleared his gruff throat—"with quite so many men tonight?"

"Yes, but I much prefer dancing here with you right now." Her legs wobbled. Was Ashten truly going to kiss her? Perhaps he was simply testing her, to see if she really did have a suitor she intended on eloping with. If he was, then she'd have to take great care.

"There's an allure to a disrespectful kiss. Do you want to know what it is?" He leaned in closer, his breath whispering across her lips.

"Tell me." She sucked in a breath, her heartbeat thundering in her ears.

"It's called the danger that awaits with the conclusion of that kiss. Does one simply stop, or does one continue with a second disrespectful kiss?"

Chapter 7

Ashten barely held his restraint in check. From the second he'd stepped inside the gazebo with Ellie, he'd known he'd be holding her in his arms before he could allow her to leave. She'd captivated him tonight, as well as sent every sound and reasonable thought disappearing right from his head. "Are you ready?" he asked her, far beyond ready himself.

"I am." She swiped her tongue across her lips and dampened them in the way a woman did right before she wished to be kissed, and her golden eyes, they shimmered all bright and beautiful, her hand trembling in his. "Please, Ashten, kiss me."

Never had he felt so alive as he did in this moment. Over the years, he'd taken the odd mistress or casual lover wherever possible, women who'd always held golden tresses and pouty lips, only not one of his lovers had ever been her—Lady Ellie Marie Trentbury. Never would they be either.

He lowered his head and unable to hold back a second longer, covered her mouth with his and kissed her, just as he'd always wished to kiss her. He licked across the seam of her lips and when she gasped, he slipped his tongue between those delectable lips and stroked across her tongue. "Come closer," he murmured against her lips.

"We're already quite close." Although she arched her back and pressed her breasts firmer into his chest, her breath mingling so seductively with his.

"That's perfect." Gently, he sucked on her indecently full lower lip then indulged in his desires and kissed her deeper.

"Oh my." She dug her fingers into his shoulders and his passion rose powerfully, just as hers did too. "I can't believe we're kissing."

"Neither can I." He pushed her up against the gazebo wall and hands sliding under the jacket he'd given her, he caressed down her sides and roamed over her lush bottom.

"Ashten?" Her breathing escalated. "I feel so much."

"Pierce."

Her wide eyes searched his. "That's your first name?"

"Yes, Pierce Luke Blackgale." Harry was the only other who knew it, particularly since he'd come into his title early in life and had always been known as Ashten.

She smiled and firmed her grip on his shoulders. "Would you please kiss me again, Pierce?"

"For as long as you desire."

"That could be for a while. I'm quite enjoying this disrespectful kiss."

"So am I." He took her mouth again and kissed her deeply, and in return she threw herself into their kiss with the same fierce ardor that took him. Her tongue danced with his in an erotic duel, her ability to kiss so intimately coming naturally to her. This was heaven, glorious heaven. He squeezed her shapely bottom, which seemed to be covered in nothing underneath the sheer layer of chiffon other than her bare skin. He certainly sensed no drawers beneath the fine fabric and his cock rose to attention and pushed determinedly against his trousers.

"Mmm," she murmured and rolled her hips against his hips. "This kind of kissing could get quite addictive."

He growled rough and low. "Disrespectful kisses can also get quickly out of hand."

"So I see, and I'm currently in approval of them. Tell me

this is real."

"This is real." He released her bottom and cupped her breasts below the neckline of her gown. He lifted her bosom higher, until the upper swells showed then he dipped his head and buried his face in the creamy mounds. "This is exactly why Winterly should be keeping a closer eye on you. I could be any man about to take advantage of you."

"But you're not just any man." She swept her hand under his chin and lifted his gaze back to hers, then ever so gently, she caressed his lips with one finger. "I never knew this kind of kissing existed."

"There can be so much more than this." He buried his face in her neck next, then kissed her soft skin as her enticing rose fragrance wafted around him. "Close your eyes, Ellie."

"What for?"

"Just close them."

"All right." She did exactly as he asked and he kneaded her breasts gently over the burgundy fabric of her gown before swiping his thumbs over her beaded nipples poking through. She let out a soft sigh, one which hardened his cock even further. "Pierce, no one has ever made me feel like this before."

"What you're feeling is the rapture that can come at having a man's hands on you." He captured her mouth again, plundered and explored to his heart's desire, until she moaned into his mouth and hell, he burned for her, wished desperately that he could peel her gown away and strip his own clothes off.

"I'm wondering if that rapture is only possible at your hand." She fingered the cravat at his neck while she nibbled on his lower lip, then she worked his neckcloth loose, the ends dangling down his chest as she stroked the skin she'd exposed. "You have a lovely neck, Your Grace."

"Take the skin of my neck into your mouth and suck on it."

"Pardon?"

"Do it."

"As you wish." She moved to do his bidding, pressed her lips to his sensitive skin and sucked on it. He moaned and pressed her harder into the gazebo wall and after a blissful minute, she finally released his skin with a little giggle and a gasp. "Oh my, I've left quite a large red mark behind. Exactly how will you explain that to your valet?"

"No one will see it but me." He stroked a finger down her neck and along the upper swells of her breasts. "Do you mind if I mark you here?"

"You wish to suck on my, ah, bosom, just as I just sucked on your neck?" She clapped a hand over her mouth. "That sounded rather indecent."

"It is. Have I shocked you with my request?"

"You have, yet I like that you did."

"Then allow me to shock you some more." He caught her hand, lowered it to his crotch and wrapped it around the rather sizable bulge she'd currently stirred to life in his trousers. "This is what you've done to me, made me harden and hunger for far more than just your kisses alone."

"What's this called?"

"A penis, or a cock."

"It's firm, and rather large. This is clearly quite a state you're in."

He couldn't help but smile. "Ellie, when two people kiss as disrespectfully as we've just done, then a man's cock can lengthen and broaden. When that happens, you're in trouble."

"Why am I in trouble?"

He moved her hand up and down over his length and hell, her innocent touch felt so agonizingly good. "It means the man you've kissed is mere minutes away from pushing his cock between your legs."

"Oh." Her eyes went saucer-wide. "Oh, I see."

He gritted his teeth to keep from coming right there and then in his pants. Devil take it. He was certainly tempted to take her hand and push it inside his waistband, only instead he managed to find some self-control, released her and stepped back as far as the opposite wall of the gazebo allowed. Trying to catch his breath, he gulped air. "It would pay for you to never ask me for a disrespectful kiss again, not unless I have the right to give it to you, which I never will. You are an innocent lady, and one I've now unfortunately taken advantage of. Call me a rake if you will. I've certainly just acted like one."

"Then what would you call me for kissing you so ferociously in return?"

"You are still an innocent lady." He kept his voice firm as he motioned to the Atkinson's rear gardens. "You should return to your brother, immediately, and without any further diversion."

"Yes, yes I should." She dipped her gaze to the ground but remained right where she was. After several seconds had passed, she lifted her gaze back to his. "I would dearly love it if you paid a call on me."

"That isn't happening." Best he lay it out straight. "You'll never be my wife."

"So nothing has changed between us after what we've just done?"

"No. I still prefer my self-exile."

She went quiet again, her gaze this time moving to the fishpond rippling with moonlight only a few feet away. A good minute passed, then two, before she slowly faced him again. "You are a contradiction. You kiss me, tell me your first name, then demand I stay away and all in the name of your self-exile."

"You are about to elope with another man in case you've forgotten, unless you spoke a mistruth to me. Is that what's happened?"

"Truthfully"—she breathed deep, her eyes a soulful golden hue—"Sophia and Olivia will one day wish to wed, and Sophia truly is smitten with James Hargrove. Winterly has also told me that I have too much love to give and would never be content as a spinster. He and Mama would also prefer I accept the next proposal I receive, which means unfortunately, I'm running out of time. That is the absolute truth."

"Don't run off to Gretna Green on some stupid whim."

"Stupid whims can sometimes turn out to be quite enjoyable, as I've just learnt tonight." A soft smile tugged at her lips. "Don't you think so?"

"No, all they do is confuse matters. I shouldn't have kissed you."

"Don't say that." Her smile disappeared.

"It's true." He pulled farther away, crossed his arms and tapped one foot. "You should leave."

"Yes, I suppose I should." She softly sighed, removed his jacket and laid it on the bench before collecting the glove he'd removed. "Thank you for my disrespectful kiss, Pierce. I'll never forget it."

Neither would he, unfortunately.

Chapter 8

Ellie awoke the next morning with a heavy head and an equally heavy heart. She pushed her lilac bedcovers away and slipped out from underneath the lacy canopy of her four-poster. Last night, Ashten had kissed her then told her she'd never be his wife, right before warning her to stay away. At the time, she'd gone from the heights of ecstasy then dropped into the sheer depths of despair. Goodness, but she had adored his kisses, had desperately wanted even more, but his words had made the ultimate sense. Stupid whims could confuse matters. Particularly when all she now desired was him, and he didn't desire her at all. How unfortunate, yet also it was now her reality, which she needed to accept. Friends, they would always be. Never anything more.

"Good morning, my lady." Penny entered with a large vase of overflowing flowers, a radiance of classic pink roses, fragrant lilies, cerise germini, and a white spray of chrysanthemums. Her maid set the vase on the nightstand, plucked a sealed card from within the fragrant blooms and handed it to her. "These just arrived for you."

"Oh my, how lovely." Could these be from Ashten? Had he possibly changed his mind and sent this peace offering in apology? Her fingers shook as she studied the wax seal. Hmm, the emblem emblazoned upon it wasn't from Ashten's ring, but instead from the House of Bishophale. Captain Poole resided at Major Lord Bishophale's residence while at home on leave. She lifted the seal, unfolded the card and read the elegantly written words.

My delightful Ellie,
The weather is radiant today and I would be honored if I could call upon you for a ride in the park. I'll pack a picnic lunch, which we can both enjoy in the sunshine. Be ready at ten.
Fondly,
Bradley.

"Open the drapes, Penny."

Her maid swished them open and Ellie pushed her bedcovers aside and smiled as sunshine poured into her chamber. Yes, it was most certainly a fine day. She set the card on her nightstand and stood at the window. The deep green foliage of the trees swayed in the gentle breeze, while birds fluttered about. The red and white roses blooming over the arbor were a bright splash of color, the yellow daisies dotting the lush grass either side of Mama's well-tended garden beds, proof that spring had most certainly arrived. Ten? Well, she didn't have long to ready herself, and she had promised Bradley a ride in the park on the next fine day. That was clearly today, and she certainly wouldn't be turning him away when he knocked on her door. She forced any residual gloominess aside since no good ever came from wallowing.

She would embrace the wonders of this new day.

She had her family close at hand, love bursting forth within these walls, and even though Harry was fighting across the channel, he was a strong officer and wouldn't wish to be anywhere else other than ensuring they remained safe here in England.

She'd also successfully gotten Ashten out of his home to

attend his club. Not quite the social setting she'd hoped for his return amongst the *ton*, but still a wonderful start.

Yes, she would have a lovely picnic in the park today with Bradley. Their competitive natures were a wonderful match, and for certain they'd have a fine time together. She didn't doubt it.

"What would you like to wear today, my lady?" Penny held two day dresses in hand.

"I'm to join Captain Poole for a picnic in the park, so I'll need my royal blue riding habit." She bustled across to her maid. "You'll be required to chaperone me. Ensure the groomsman readies my mare for me, and the curricle for you."

"Of course." Her maid hung the dresses and pulled out her riding habit and a broad-brimmed hat.

She tugged her nightgown over her head, donned her chemise, then slipped the white blouse Penny handed her on over top. Fitted jacket next, buttoned to her neck. The riding habit's skirts were long and full, cumbersome and a little weighty, but the thicker layer would keep her warm outside should the weather turn. She sat on the end of her bed and laced her leather boots, while Penny popped down to the kitchens.

Her maid returned with a breakfast tray, and she sat at her side table and enjoyed a delicious helping of scrambled eggs and toasted bread slathered in butter.

With her matching royal blue hat atop her head, her hair secured at the sides with two pins and her locks swaying down her back, she left her room and skipped downstairs.

"You have loud footsteps." With a knowing smile, Winterly emerged from his study and eyed her. "And you appear rather chipper. Is this to do with the bouquet that arrived for you this morning?"

"Yes. I'm joining Captain Poole for a ride in the park, as well as a picnic lunch since the sun is finally out again." She certainly didn't wish to waste another minute of this day by remaining indoors, not now she'd made the decision to embrace all the possibilities it held. "Did you wish to join us?" Her brother would never tag along, but she asked all the same. "I've no issue if you do."

"If you're taking Penny as your chaperone, then I'll remain right here." He pulled her into his arms and hugged her, his tan trousers pressed and his matching jacket flowing smoothly over his broad shoulders. "I'm also in a meeting, which has not long begun."

"With Mr. Tidmore?" She'd love to say hello to her current cohort if he was here.

"No, and brace yourself." Winterly gripped her hands, his gaze focused. "It's Ashten."

"Pardon?" She swayed, black dots dancing in front of her eyes.

"Good morning, Lady Ellie." Cane in hand, Ashten stepped out of her brother's study in buff breeches which molded his strong thighs, his riding boots buckled an inch below his knees.

Was the Duke of Ashten truly here, or was she simply imagining him?

"I, ah..." She stepped up to her vision of Ashten and gently laid one hand on his jacketed arm. Definite warmth penetrated through to her fingers. She stared at him, unable to look anywhere else. "Oh my, you're truly real. Has Mama seen you?"

"You didn't hear her piercing screech an hour ago?" A teasing smile shone in his eyes. He wanted to be here, had been enjoying his visit with her brother thus far. That was clear to see.

"No, and if she hears you speak about her like that, she'll clap your ears, whether you're a duke or not."

"I'd expect naught less from her."

Winterly chuckled and tweaked her nose. "I'd wondered if we'd been invaded by the French when I entered the foyer earlier and discovered it was merely Ashten's arrival that had caused Mama to cry."

"Where is she now?"

"With Sophia and Olivia. They still required masks for the Campton's War Society Charity Masquerade Ball. They gushed over the arrival of your flowers earlier, and Mama expected you might be busy. The three of them snuck away a few minutes ago."

"I already have my costume and mask." She lowered her hand from Ashten's arm since she was still touching him, her shock slowly subsiding. "It's truly wonderful you're here."

"I received a business proposition from your brother in this morning's mail and on a *whim*, decided to investigate it further. A maritime venture with an American shipping merchant named Mr. Tidmore. He'll be arriving to join in our meeting soon." He moved his cane to his left hand and with his right, lifted her hand and pressed a kiss across her gloved knuckles. "You look bright and radiant this morning."

"I wish I'd known you were coming. I might've been able to change my plans if I did."

"I wouldn't have expected you to. You should enjoy your ride and picnic in the park."

A knock rattled the front door and Penny opened it.

Mr. Tidmore stepped inside wearing dark trousers and a navy waistcoat, a black jacket folded over his arm. He dipped his head and took her hand with a flourish. "My lovely, Lady Ellie. You look ravishing on this fine spring day."

"It's lovely to see you too." She gestured to Ashten. "Mr. Tidmore, I'd like to introduce you to the Duke of Ashten."

"Yes, I've been looking forward to meeting you." Mr. Tidmore extended his hand to Ashten. "Lady Ellie has spoken about you often, Winterly too, of your great service in the war and your deep friendship with their family. It's an honor to finally meet you."

"Call me Ashten." He shook Tidmore's hand. "Winterly and I have been speaking in depth about your shipping ventures."

"Wonderful. We require one more financial partner in order to undertake the future ventures we wish to progress with, and I've requested the accounts be sent over here to Winterly today. They should arrive later this afternoon." Mr. Tidmore cast his gaze back to her. "I had hoped to see you today as well, to ask if you might be available for an evening at one of the playhouses on Drury Lane? Lord Marriweather and his wife have invited me to join them in their box tomorrow night."

"I'd be honored to attend a play with you tomorrow night."

"Excellent. Then I'll collect you here at six. Lady Marriweather mentioned the two of you were second cousins."

"Yes, on Mama's side of the family. Lady Marriweather and I had our first Season together, then she met Viscount Marriweather on her second Season and the two wed before the end of that year."

"They're a delightful couple."

The clip-clop of horses' hooves echoed from outside and Penny opened the front door just as Captain Poole handed his reins to the groom and strode up the driveway.

"Good morning, one and all." Poole stepped inside and nodded at Winterly, Ashten, and Mr. Tidmore, then swept into an elegant bow before her, his tailcoats swaying. "And a good morning to you, my delightful companion for the day. My cook has prepared us a picnic to enjoy."

"Thank you for the flowers. They're immensely beautiful."

"As is the lady I sent them to."

Heat flushed her cheeks, and Winterly cleared his throat with a barely contained grunt of laughter. If her brother could, he would likely be rubbing his hands together in glee right now. Three eligible gentlemen stood within only a few feet of her, his every dream come true.

"Let's be away, shall we?" Captain Poole extended his arm to her and she slipped her hand through the crook and blew her brother a kiss. "Enjoy your business meeting today." To Mr.

Tidmore, she said, "Tomorrow night at six." And to Ashten, she murmured, "You are like family to us and should visit more often. Don't allow another six months to pass before you do."

"Yes, my lady." A dark scowl furrowed Ashten's brow as he eyed Poole. "Hyde Park, is it?"

"Yes." Poole cast his gaze to Winterly. "My lord, I'll return your sister to you by three this afternoon. Will that suffice?"

"Only if you must." Her brother's eyes danced with mischief. "Our Ellie is a handful, which is the only warning I'm going to give you. Do enjoy your picnic."

"It's my brother who's actually the handful. Ignore his warning." She smiled sweetly at Poole while her brother asked Mr. Tidmore and Ashten to join him in his study. She hurried the captain out the door, while Ashten remained in the foyer watching her leave with his scowl still in place.

Outside on the driveway, Poole drew her to a stop and patted her hand. "Wait right here while I transfer the picnic basket into your maid's curricle. I'll bring your mare to you right after."

"Thank you."

Poole left her side and saw the basket handed over from his man who'd ridden with him to her driver, then he aided Penny into the curricle and disappeared into the stables to collect her mare from one of their liveried grooms.

"Is he the one?" Ashten murmured in a low voice from behind her.

She jumped, clutching a hand to her chest. "Ashten, you gave me a surprise."

"Last night, after you left, all I could think about was how I pushed you away with my harsh words. I apologize profusely, Ellie." Sadness haunted his blue eyes. "Will you forgive me?"

"Yes, absolutely." Mama had taught her to never hold a grudge, and Ashten was Harry's best friend, a man she considered a friend too, that's if a lady were permitted male friends.

"So, I see Poole sent you flowers this morning, and Tidmore is to enjoy an evening out with you tomorrow night. You seem to have a number of suitors flittering about you."

"There is only one suitor who matters."

"Yes, the one you intend on eloping with." He gently touched his knuckles to her cheek, his sadness deepening as he drew them slowly away. "Enjoy your day, my sweet."

"I shall. You enjoy yours too."

"I would enjoy it more if I had you to gaze upon within Winterly's study, rather than your brother." A soft smile, then he turned and disappeared inside, the front door clicking shut behind him.

Her heart ached for him, for them both. If only he actually did desire her, then she'd be walking right back inside after him. No hesitation.

"Here we are." Poole walked her mare toward her.

"I'm looking forward to this ride. It feels like an age since I last felt the sunshine on my face."

"So that's where these delightful freckles have come from?" Smiling warmly, Poole touched her cheek with one finger.

"I'm afraid so. I'm wearing a hat today, but I can't guarantee it'll remain atop my head the entire day."

"Then I'll keep an eye on your wayward hat, and return it to you if it dares to fly away." He clasped her waist and lifted her into her saddle then mounted his own horse and with Penny already seated in the curricle beside her driver, she pressed her knees into her mount's sides and trotted alongside the captain as the sun shone high above.

Towering trees lined each side of the street, the lush green front gardens hiding stately homes in the rear. Poole doffed his hat at Lady Allingsworth and her eldest daughter who'd chosen to enjoy a stroll to the shops rather than to take a carriage for the short walk. The day was simply too fine to be confined inside a chariot, and the ladies offered charming smiles to Poole in return.

"Are you enjoying your time on leave?" she asked Poole as birds twittered from up high in their nests. A dog barked down a driveway, and a cat skittered up the closest tree.

"It's always a relief to set my weapons aside and not worry over what battle I must fight the next day." Posture tall and strong, his reins held firmly in hand, he skimmed their surroundings as if on alert. "Yet even with that relief, there is still a sense of unease that consumes me. Each morning when I awaken, I fear what news might come through the War Office."

"It is a great service you undertake for your country." She moved with the gentle gait of her mare. "I can't say that enough."

"My brother's betrothed said the same words to me this morning, which are touching to hear. You have my thanks for saying so as well."

"Which of your brothers is now betrothed?" His eldest brother, Lord Major Bishophale, had wed several years ago and had two young sons, although she was aware Bradley had two younger brothers, twins John and Jeffery born two years after him.

"John is now engaged to the delightful Miss Sarah Shepherd. He's actually riding to Dover tomorrow to take some papers to Lieutenant Colonel Masters, so while he's away I've promised to escort my future sister-in-law about town."

"That is wonderful of you."

"John would've had my hide if I hadn't offered to show her about town, particularly since she's new to London, and honestly, it is a privilege to be in her company. She is such a delight." They broke free of the cover of trees lining the busy street and the sun glimmered across her companion's golden hair under the brim of his hat, his locks cropped short as many of the officers preferred. Harry had sported the exact same hairstyle on his last bout of leave nine months ago.

"I don't believe I've met Miss Shepherd before." Her name didn't ring any bells.

"You possibly wouldn't have. Her family live farther to the north. Nottingham to be exact."

"Then how ever did Miss Shepherd and your brother meet?" A gentleman strolling along the side walk hailed a hack and she steered her horse around him and the conveyance.

"John was passing through Nottingham a few months ago, and when he fell ill he sought shelter at an inn, one Miss Shepherd's father was called to tend him at. Mr. Shepherd is a physician, and his daughter is his rather skilled aide. I can only say Miss Shepherd nursed John through a severe fever and afterward, well, it was love at first sight. She is now a guest at Bishophale House, enjoying the Season before it ends."

"Hopefully, I'll get the chance to meet her while she's in town then."

"I'll make certain that happens."

"I'll hold you to that." She breathed deep as they rode along the busier streets and the welcome sounds of the town surrounded her.

Another mile or two later, they passed underneath one of the three carriage entrance archways and entered the park. The long length of the Serpentine weaved through hundreds of acres of royal parkland, this place a popular gathering ground and her fingers itched to give her horse its head, to enjoy a faster pace with the wind rushing through her hair, just as it usually did when she rode at Winterly Manor in the country.

"Do you feel like a race?" Poole smiled knowingly at her, as if he too wished to let loose and ride like the wind.

"Yes, I'd love a race."

"To the lake's edge then, where the large oak sits," he instructed her. "Do you know the spot?"

"Yes, of course."

"Excellent." He cast a glance over his shoulder and shouted the same instructions to the driver, that they were to race to the lake and to follow them as they were able.

Oh goodness. She'd need at least a minute or two's head start if she wished to win this race. She thrust her knees into her mare's sides and bolted, then keeping her head tucked close to her horse's neck, she weaved through the trees and galloped across the grassy meadow, the pounding of horse's hooves thundering close behind her.

"You cheat!" Poole caught up to her with a laugh, his eyes bright and his hat tucked under one arm so it didn't fly off. His stallion snorted air, his sleek black coat gleaming in the sunshine. They were magnificent, man and beast both.

"I thought you told me to start."

"I did no such thing."

"You're supposed to say you did. A lady is never wrong."

Another burst of laughter. "I see your competitive nature follows you from the dancefloor to the countryside."

"It follows me everywhere I go." She laughed too, the silk ties of her hat fluttering under her chin. "Although I won't be shown up without a fight."

"What if I give you to the count of ten before I give the call for our actual race to begin."

"That sounds perfect." She snapped her reins, lunged forward and rode as fast as her horse could carry her. Under tree limbs, she ducked, then jumped the odd log. Poole caught up to her within a mere minute then passed right by and drat it all, the captain disappeared through the bushes up ahead and when she finally cleared the woods and the lake's grassy edge loomed up ahead, the ancient oak tree with its wide boughs reaching toward the sky, he'd already tethered his horse to a branch and laid on the grass with his arms crossed behind his head as if he'd been whiling away the day for hours.

Cheeks hot, she jumped to the ground and looped her reins loosely around the branch next to his, her mare easily able to reach the water for a drink.

Breathlessly, she dropped onto the grass beside Poole and giggled. "Well, you won that race fair and square."

"The first win of many races to come, I hope." Grinning, he rolled onto his side and propped his head into his cupped palm. "You're a delight to be around, Ellie, like a ray of sunshine that spreads its warmth to all those close at hand."

"You are too kind."

More hoofbeats thundered beyond the bushes and she snuck a look over her shoulder just as a horse and rider tore out of the woods, the big black beast a thoroughbred for certain, the rider holding a sleek mane of dark shoulder-length hair and a white shirt billowing in the breeze. The rider's piercing blue gaze captured hers and her heartbeat pounded. "Oh my."

"Well, well." A nostalgic smile from the captain. "It appears the Duke of Ashten is no longer in self-exile."

"Yes, and it's wonderful to see." She wanted to clap and shout her excitement. "It also appears we're about to be interrupted."

"It does. I'll go and ask Ashten if he wishes to join us, particularly since it appears that's his current intention." Poole rose and ambled across to Ashten, then shook his hand and gestured for the duke to join them.

Ashten looped his reins around a branch as she and Poole had done, then he unstrapped his cane and limped across. Standing over her, he pulled his riding gloves off, pocketed them and eyed her speculatively. "It's such a beautiful day that I decided to take a ride in the park. I wasn't sure I'd even come across you and Poole, what with the hundreds of acres where you could have hidden."

"We're not hiding."

"You're without a chaperone."

"Penny won't be far away, and we indulged in a race, which is why I'm currently without her." The clatter of the curricle's wheels over the uneven ground echoed through the trees. "See, there she is."

"I'll fetch the blanket and basket I brought." Poole strode across the thick grass and disappeared beyond the bushes.

"Ellie?" Ashten lowered to a crouch, set his cane on the ground next to her and gently tucked a loose lock of her hair behind her ear, his gaze locked tight with hers.

"Yes?"

He gulped, his throat working and worry flickering in his eyes.

"Is something wrong?"

"No, but you have the most adorable ears, and the most adorable nose too. Have I ever told you that?"

"No." Her belly fluttered, although she sternly told herself not to let his words mean anything more than what they were.

"You've the most beguiling golden eyes and pouty lips as well."

"Oh." Perhaps he did mean more.

"Don't go to the playhouse with Mr. Tidmore, or out on another ride with Poole." A firm look in his eyes.

"Is there a reason why I shouldn't, Your Grace?"

"Pierce." His gaze narrowed. "Say my name. I love it when you do, particularly all breathy and with need blazing in your eyes."

"I've never said your name in such a way."

"Yes, you have, in my rear gardens, near the fishpond, within my gazebo under a moonlit sky. We danced. We kissed. You called me Pierce, and I wanted to devour you." He traced a finger over her lower lip. "All I've dreamed about since that moment is kissing you again."

"Yet you also told me at the time that you don't wish for a wife. Does that remain the case?" Hope flickered in her heart.

"No, I've still no desire for one."

Chapter 9

Voices traveled through the bushes, that of Ellie's maid and Captain Poole. Ashten rose from his crouch next to Ellie and accepted the blanket Poole held out to him. He spread the blue and white tartan out and offered Ellie a hand to scoot onto it, while her maid remained near the horses, affording them suitable privacy while still keeping them in her sight.

Ellie tugged the ribbons holding her hat in place and set it beside her, then pulled the pins from either side of her head and ran her fingers through her golden locks, which cascaded down her back in a glorious fall of soft waves.

"Do you care for some red wine?" Poole removed a bottle from his picnic basket and held out the bottle for Ellie's examination.

"Oh, yes, please. Let me find the glasses." She rummaged through the basket and extended them as Poole poured. "I don't believe I've seen that marker on a wine bottle before. It appears to be the letter S enclosed within a laurel wreath."

"This bottle is from a delightful vineyard I found in Spain. I wished to bring an entire case back after first sampling it, but with my need to travel light, unfortunately I couldn't." Poole slipped the bottle back in the basket, then accepted the glass Ellie handed him.

She sipped delicately from her stemmed flute. "Mmm, it's

delicious."

Hell, naught was more obvious that this was a date for two. This outing, in every way, rung of a courtship. Ellie and Poole had enjoyed a ride through the park and the captain had even packed a bottle of his favorite wine, the only bottle he'd brought all the way back with him from Spain. Good grief. Why the blazes had he followed her and his comrade here? Yes, he'd been driven to, had been immensely worried that Poole was indeed the man she intended on eloping with, but there was far more to it than that. Since the moment his Ellie had forced her way into his bedchamber, his good sense had completely deserted him.

"Would you like to try some?" Holding out her glass, Ellie smiled at him.

"I'm not thirsty, but thank you all the same." He should leave and let them enjoy their date. Poole was a good man, would keep her safe should he be the one about to elope with her.

"You must be thirsty after your ride." She waved the glass in front of his nose this time, a teasing glimmer lighting her eyes. "Or are you scared of sharing my glass?"

"That is an absurd thing to say." Jaw clenched, he accepted the glass and sipped from the same spot along the rim as she had. Three was a crowd, and he was most definitely the third in their crowd. He truly should leave.

"Mmm, I'm famished too." Ellie peeked inside the basket then withdrew several cut sandwiches and removed the wrappings. "It appears we have roast beef and tomato, or chicken and cheese sandwiches. What would you like, Bradley?"

"You choose first," Poole offered with a tender smile, which he wanted to wipe from his friend's face with his fist. While he'd had to demand Ellie call him by his first name, she seemed to have no issue letting loose with Poole's first name, here, there, and everywhere.

"Chicken and cheese for me then." She set her sandwich on

a plate and handed Poole two of the others on another plate, before offering Ashten a couple of beef sandwiches. "Don't tell me you're not hungry."

He didn't, but instead muttered, "Thank you."

Facing his foe again, his Ellie smiled ever so brightly. "Bradley, I'd love to hear all about Spain, about the people there. What are they like?"

"They're resilient and strong, and even though their battle against Napoleon isn't done, they'll never allow the Corsican to take their country."

"I fear for them."

"As we all do. Liberation Napoleon calls it, but the Spanish people have a very crafty way of dealing with him. Ambushes, sabotage, and raids. It's all been rather refreshing fighting at their side and seeing their tactics firsthand."

"Everywhere the Corsican goes he wreaks carnage. At times, I can barely stomach hearing his name." She bit into her sandwich then gently laid her hand on Ashten's arm while keeping her gaze on Poole. Her comforting move twisted his heart and made him long for her all over again. She understood him so damn well, how soul-destroying fighting in Spain had been for him and even though conversing with another man, she'd reached out to him to offer him her unequivocal support.

Poole cleared his throat. "The Spanish people love their land too much to ever allow it to be taken by another."

"I do wonder why Napoleon ever believed they'd welcome him onto their soil." She sipped her wine. "Regardless of the war though, I'm told Spain is beautiful."

"Its beauty is certainly undeniable. Stunning beaches, charming countryside, and fertile vineyards with the best wine on offer." Poole crossed his ankles as he cast his gaze out over the rippling waters of the Serpentine. "But of course, there is also plenty of devastation too."

"At least we've been able to maintain our ability to trade

with the Spanish." Another bite of her sandwich.

"Agreed. None of us will permit Napoleon to fully destroy their fine country."

Footsteps crunched through the leaf-strewn grass and the driver of Ellie's curricle strode around the bushes and halted before the captain, a folded note in one hand. "Excuse me, sir, but a rider just handed me this missive from Major Lord Bishophale and he now awaits your response at the curricle. The man isn't permitted to leave without one."

"Let me see it." Poole accepted the note and broke the seal. He scanned the missive, a frown furrowing his brow.

"Is all well?" Ellie's voice hitched with worry.

"The War Office is requesting my brother and I attend an urgent meeting and Bishophale has already ridden for the Horse Guards in Whitehall. He conveys the need for me to join him there immediately."

"Then you must leave."

"Yes, I'm so sorry to be bringing our delightful day to an end." Poole patted Ellie's hand. "I can see you safely home first, have no fear there."

"You'll have to ride out of your way to take me home. No, I shall simply hold you up. I can make my own way home. My maid and driver will see me safely back."

"I can see the lady home if you wish." Ashten would never allow Ellie to make her own way home, whether Poole conceded his agreement or not.

"You have my thanks, Ashten. I shall most certainly take you up on that offer." Poole rose to his feet, bowed curtly over Ellie. "I shall make this up to you. I give you my word I will."

"Think nothing of it."

"Finish the wine. There is no need for it to go to waste. I pray you will enjoy your day."

"Ride safely."

"I shall." Poole loped across to his horse, mounted and with a wave, charged through the woods.

"I hope all is well at the War Office." Ellie gripped his arm. "What would cause his brother to send such an urgent message to him?"

"There could be a number of reasons, but don't fear over what they might be. Bishophale and Poole will have things in hand. They are well versed in this war."

"Yes, I know you're right, but I've always been such a worrywart." She went quiet, very quiet, which was most unlike his Ellie.

"I truly shall see you safely home, and if you want to leave now, simply say so and we can be on our way."

"No, I'd rather sit here and enjoy this fine day." Her frown receded and she pulled away and busied herself riffling through the basket once more. "Oh, look at this. We have apricots."

"I love apricots."

"I'll feed you." Smiling, she held one to his lips. "Open your mouth."

"I'm not five. I can feed myself, thank you very much."

"Of course you can, but will that be any fun?" She arched a challenging brow. "I insist."

"I detest it when you insist." Still, he opened his mouth and when she popped the apricot between his lips, he snapped his mouth over both the fruit and her fingers.

She giggled. "You can be so playful at times. I'd forgotten that."

"You can be too trusting."

"Do you remember that day when I followed you and Harry back to Blackgale Park and you and my brother raided the apricot tree?"

"Harry and I filled a large pail each then took our haul down to the stream. We ate until our bellies bulged." That day would forever be etched in his memory.

"Yes, and you and Harry both looked quite ill afterward."

"Harry said I couldn't eat as many apricots as him. I had to prove him wrong."

"You two only offered me one apricot from each of your pails. I thought that most unfair."

"We didn't want to spoil your appetite before dinner."

"No, you didn't want to share." Her golden eyes sparkled, her smile wide. "Let me make another dare now, on behalf of Harry since he isn't here."

"You want to see who can eat the most apricots from that basket?"

"No, I wish to dare you to come to the Campton's War Society Charity Masquerade Ball, and while you're there, to sign your name on my dance card."

He was tempted, incredibly tempted. "That kind of a dare should go two ways."

"Name your dare and I'll honor it."

"Send your maid away right now." What the hell was he doing asking that?

"That's your dare?"

"Yes."

"But I can't do that. We'd be left alone and if anyone saw us, there'd be talk, then you'd be honor bound to offer for me, and we both know you don't wish to take me as your wife. Your words, not mine."

"This spot is completely secluded." Gah, he needed to shut his mouth.

She glanced about, her brows pinched together as if she was actually considering his dare, then she called out to Penny, "Take a walk if you like, but don't let the groomsman see you wandering about."

"Are you sure, my lady?"

"Yes, very sure. The duke is like a brother to me, and we wish to speak in private."

"As you wish." Her maid dutifully bobbed her head and

disappeared into the trees.

"Done." Ellie brushed her hands together, looking incredibly gleeful as she did.

"I'd rather you ceased comparing me to Harry." Particularly since his current thoughts were anything other than brotherly. He wanted her underneath him, her beautiful bosom exposed to his hands and his mouth on her luscious nipples.

"You're not wheedling your way out of this dare. I expect to see you at the masquerade, and to have my dance. I'm also not giving away what my costume shall be, or the mask I shall wear. You will have to do your very best to find me." She unbuttoned her royal blue riding jacket and laid it on the grass beside her. "The day is warming up beautifully."

"You are such a scamp." There would be hundreds of costumed people in the ballroom and even if he did decide to accept her dare and attend, he might never be able to find her.

"Yes, but you've always known that." She held out another apricot. "Care for another bite, Your Grace."

"You are riding the fine line of trouble between us." So was he. He crossed his arms behind his head, settled on his back and opened his mouth. Gads, why couldn't he halt his atrocious behavior? "Feed me."

"No mischief this time." She leaned over him, pressed the apricot to his lips, the scalloped neckline of her white blouse dipping and exposing the upper swells of her breasts, the lacy chemise underneath barely containing them.

"I like making mischief." He spread his hands around her waist to keep her close, then he bit into the succulent fruit, his gaze on hers and his heartbeat thundering in his ears. "What am I going to do with you, Ellie Marie?"

"Perhaps offer me another disrespectful kiss?"

Not on his life would he do that.

He was already in deep enough trouble.

Chapter 10

Ellie fed Ashten another apricot, wishing like crazy he truly did wish for her to be his wife, except he'd declared well and true he didn't desire such a union, and far more than once. Still, she would enjoy her day, and this precious time she'd been gifted with him. She tossed the pip, nabbed yet another apricot from the basket and this time bit into the succulent fruit herself. "It's at times like these," she murmured as she licked her lips of the apricot juice, "that I miss Harry dreadfully."

"Why is that?" Ashten lifted up then shockingly, actually settled his head in her lap as he laid back down again.

"What are you doing?"

"Resting, and I like it when you feed me. Please, don't stop." He caught her hand and drew the apricot she'd bitten into, down to his mouth. Another bite, another naughty grin, then he released her hand and closed his eyes. With a yawn, he stretched and made himself even more comfortable, his hair lifting in the gentle breeze and fluttering against her royal blue skirts. "Tell me why you miss Harry."

"Whenever you and I have been together in the past, so has Harry."

"Yes, I agree. Your lap is extremely comfortable, by the way."

"You're fortunate I sent my maid away. She would be

flabbergasted by your current behavior." Sunshine dappled across his high cheeks and strong jaw, the breeze stirring the lush foliage overhead and swishing it about. The water of the Serpentine rippled and lapped into shore, the grassy bank so close that if she wiggled a toe, she might even be able to reach the water's edge with it, or if she wiggled and bent over, she might be able to touch her lips to Ashten's, and not fleetingly either. No, she still wished to kiss him as disrespectfully as he'd kissed her in his garden, and she doubted she'd ever not wish to.

Gently, she ran her fingers through Ashten's dark locks and tidied them. So silky soft, the length reaching his shoulders, wild and free, just as the man currently was. "My suitor isn't Captain Poole." A soft admission. She couldn't help but make it.

"Then why accept Poole's invitation for a day out?"

"So you won't guess who my true beau is."

"Blast it all, Ellie." He thumped the ground, rose swiftly and tipped her onto her back on the blanket. His eyes glittered as bright as sapphires as he slid his fingers around her nape. "Damn you," he murmured, then drew her mouth closer to his.

"Are you going to kiss me again?"

"No." With a low growl, he brushed a kiss across her forehead instead of her lips.

"Pierce?" She wrapped her arms around his neck and clung to him. "Life isn't meant to be lived behind four walls."

"I'm well aware." He guided her mouth to his, urged her lips apart then kissed her, his breath whispering softly across her tongue in a teasing caress she completely adored.

"I love it when you kiss me," she murmured against his lips.

"I shouldn't be kissing you." He caressed her sides, roamed down and scooped her bottom through her skirts. Lifting her closer against him, he pressed his hips more firmly to hers. "Say, yes to another kiss."

"Yes." Butterflies took flight in her belly, his warm breath fanning her lips.

Slowly, he brushed his mouth over hers, his lips so achingly soft as he joined them together a second time. Playfully, he nipped her lower lip, sucked it into his mouth and desire swarmed her senses.

Her breasts swelled underneath the heaviness of his chest, and a sweet yet desperate sensation washed through her.

"I can't believe we're kissing." She nibbled on his lips in return and he groaned, deep and throaty before capturing her mouth and offering her a wicked kiss she'd never forget. Intense passion flooded her.

"Ellie, I love how you feel underneath me, your body so gloriously curved." He grazed a finger along the upper swells of her breasts where her blouse's neckline dipped and she squeezed her eyes shut then opened them again.

"One more kiss," she demanded.

"No, we've kissed too much as it is, and this is dangerous territory we're headed into. I followed you to make certain Poole didn't ravish you, and now here I am doing exactly that."

"What if I said I liked being ravished by you?" She certainly did. She'd never lie to him about that.

Chapter 11

Frustration pummeled through Ashten. He'd kissed Ellie yet again and truly shouldn't have, and now she'd gone and declared that she liked being ravished by him. Ugh, a diversion was needed, and fast. He eased up and put the picnic basket between them, poured her another glass of wine and handed it to her, then gulped the last few mouthfuls straight from the bottle before dropping the empty flagon inside the basket. The bottle thumped against a pack of cards in the bottom. Perfect. A game of cards would hopefully distract his amorous thoughts, and the last time they'd played together had been nine months ago after dinner one night at the Trentbury's table. Harry had played too, as well as watched on and stated how evenly matched he and Ellie had now gotten. He shuffled the deck, asked her, "Do you care for a game of stud poker?"

"I've been playing with Winterly lately, and gotten quite good at the game. What shall the stakes be?"

"The usual. The first to win ten rounds always chooses their spoils, within reason of course."

"Perfect. I'm looking forward to this." She accepted the shuffled deck and dealt their cards.

Their game began and drat it all, but Ellie had most certainly gotten quite good of late. She won ten rounds in a row and he stared at her with annoyance and muttered, "Deal again. I need to at least win one hand before this day is done."

"Of which it is almost at an end." She motioned to the sun dipping lower in the sky. "Are you even concentrating on the game, Your Grace?"

"Pierce." Hell, she appeared so ethereal sitting across from him, her voluminous riding skirts hiding her legs and her glorious golden hair swaying down her back, the ends falling into lush curls. She reminded him of a fairy, the way she sat so beguilingly with the woods on one side and the lapping waters the other.

"What's causing your current anger, Pierce?"

"You." His mind kept replaying their kisses, and how he'd much rather still be kissing her. She was full of effervescence, quick wit, and a caring and affectionate nature he'd always admired. Yes, she'd not only come to him at Blackgale House and actually managed to get him outside his front door, but she'd done so with an innocence he'd now stolen from her with his amorous kisses. He slid one hand into the pocket of his breeches and fingered the gold silk ribbon he'd tucked there this morning. Where was his good luck when he needed it? Particularly in setting her aside.

"Tell me what I can do to disperse your ill feelings then." She touched his cheek with her palm, her skin so soft and warm.

"To start with, you could at least cease looking so adorable." He scooped up the cards and stood. "Up you get. It's getting cold."

"Right then. I take it we're leaving?" She pushed to her feet and brushed her royal blue skirts. "I'll go and find Penny."

"Don't get lost while you do. I'll wait for you at the curricle with the horses. Don't be long either."

"Yes, Your Grouchiness." She chuckled and ducked his scolding look then walked off in the direction where Penny had gone when instructed to leave.

He packed the basket, folded the blanket over his arm,

collected his cane and with their horses' reins in hand, he ambled back to the groomsman and loaded everything away in the curricle.

Ellie arrived moments later with Penny, her maid having not gone too far thankfully, and after he'd aided Penny into her seat beside the driver, he gripped Ellie by the waist and lifted her into her saddle.

"Thank you." She smiled down at him from up high on her perch.

"You're welcome." Discreetly, he ran one hand along her calf under the hem of her royal blue skirts. He didn't want to step away from her, didn't want this beautiful day with her to end, didn't want to leave this magical place either. Unfortunately, he had no choice.

He mounted his stallion and they rode back to her home. In the driveway, the sun dipped below the horizon, the sky awash with a splash of red before turning a midnight-black. He bounded down from his horse, came around to Ellie and swung her down beside him. He gave her a deep, respectful bow, murmured, "I've had a delightful afternoon."

"So have I. The best in quite some time."

"I bid you a good night."

"No, you can't leave yet. I've chosen my spoils from my win, and within reason too."

"What shall those spoils be?"

"For you to come inside for dinner. Mama will be terribly upset if you leave without joining us. It's pork pie night."

"I love pork pie." And it was a fair request she'd made. He lifted his nose to the air and breathed deep, then caught the tantalizing aroma of pork wafting by. Something else as well. He sniffed again. "Is that roast beef I can smell too?"

"I'm not sure, but I trust your sense of smell. You and Harry could always scent what was for dinner before we ever entered the dining room." A smile tugged at her lips. "Please,

Pierce, come inside."

"All right." He grumbled a little, so she wouldn't think she'd won him over too easily.

Grinning, she lifted a hand to the waiting stable lad. "Brush our horses down and give them both an extra hand of oats."

"Yes, my lady."

"Thank you." She hooked her arm through the crook in his own and he escorted her inside the house, where indeed the hearty aroma of roast beef swirled through the air along with the savory scent of pork pie.

"Mama?" Ellie called out from the foyer.

"In the drawing room, my dear."

"Look who I've brought home for dinner." He got tugged into the drawing room and more squeals resounded, shrieks twice as loud as this morning when he'd arrived and been greeted by Harry's mother and sisters.

He kissed each of the ladies' hands, Sophia and Olivia's first, the ladies seated next to the crackling fire, then Lady Winterly's after she'd dropped her embroidery into the basket at her feet, her lacy cap pinned atop of her head and her smile wide. As he bowed over her hand, he asked, "Did you have a lovely day, my lady?"

"Oh, my dear boy, we certainly did, and now you've topped it off again. Don't forget, it's Flora. There's no need to stand on formality with me, as I've told you countless times before." Flora grasped his hands firmly in hers, as if she didn't wish for him to step away. "The cook has even added apple to the pork pie, and I know you love that combination well. There's roast beef as well, Yorkshire pudding and plenty of gravy. Sponge cake for dessert. I hope you're famished."

"See." Ellie cocked one brow that said she was right. He was expected.

"Now," Flora gasped as she glanced from him to Ellie, "you must explain how you came to be together. Winterly mentioned you and Poole were to enjoy a ride and picnic in the park, so there's surely a tale to tell which will explain how you left with one gentleman yet returned with another, not that I mind who you returned with of course."

"Not long after Poole and I got settled in the park near the Serpentine, Ashten joined us, then a messenger rode in with a missive from Captain Poole's brother, Major Lord Bishophale. The major asked Poole to meet him at the War Office, so he had to rush off. Thankfully, Ashten remained with me. That's how we came to be together."

"Oh dear, I do wonder what could be afoot now at the War Office."

A puppy yapped from within the folds of the blanket covering Sophia's lap.

"Shh, little one." Sophia petted its wee head. "It's all right. This is the Duke of Ashten. He's Harry's dearest friend." Sophia waved him over. "Come and meet our puppy."

"Well, it's lovely to make your acquaintance." He crouched in front of Sophia and held out his palm for the pup to smell. He got a wet lick as his reward, the puppy jumping on Sophia's skirted legs, its black and white ears flopping about, the rest of his wee body a glorious patchwork of the same two colors. The tiny thing couldn't be more than eight weeks old and could surely fit in the palm of his hand.

"He's certainly happy to see you." Sophia held the puppy out for him to take. "This is Beast, Winterly's new hunting dog, or he will be when he grows up. He's an English Springer Spaniel."

"I missed meeting Beast this morning." He hadn't heard a word about the new addition to the Trentbury household either. He rose and tucked the tiny critter in close to his jacketed chest as Ellie rubbed between Beast's ears. She dipped in and touched her nose to the pup's nose, her cheek brushing his chest and making him hunger for more of her affection too. "Where do you keep him?" he asked Ellie.

"He sleeps in Harry's room at night." She nuzzled the puppy some more, her golden locks lit an even more brilliant golden hue by the firelight. "We keep a padded basket right beside Harry's bed, so that when Harry next returns on leave, Beast will already be aware of his scent."

"Are you saying Harry's a smelly chap?"

"No, not at all." She giggled, her face flushing so delightfully. "You are so naughty."

"Not nearly as naughty as you."

She gasped, her face flushing even further. At Lady Winterly's laugh and her sisters' chuckles, Ellie shook her head at them. "That's what I mean by naughty, making outrageous comments like that. Ignore him. I am never naughty and you're all well aware of it."

"You're the naughtiest of all my children." Flora patted her chest as her laughter slowly subsided.

"Mama, if I have a touch of naughtiness within me, then it comes directly from you." She kissed her mama's cheek, Sophia and Olivia's too, then wandered to the grand piano underneath the wide window framed with blue and silver drapes, which overlooked the rear gardens. Ellie sat on the polished wooden bench seat and tapped a few keys. She warmed up then asked everyone, "What would you all like to hear while we await the maid's call for dinner?"

"Something naughty." Olivia laughed and laughed, her blond locks bouncing about her sweet cherub face and her pure white gown shimmering from the corner lamp. With only a year separating each of these sisters, Flora had certainly had her hands full, Winterly too once he'd taken his late father's title and leading place in their household. Three husbands would be needed before too long, three men who enjoyed the closeness of this family's familiar bonds.

"You are as naughty as the duke." Ellie tsked Olivia.

"Good evening, everyone." Winterly strode in with Tidmore one step behind him, then Harry's eldest brother clasped him on the shoulder. "I heard the shrieks again and knew you must have arrived. Excellent, and I see you've now met Beast."

"I have." He secured Beast closer to his chest as he shook Mr. Tidmore's hand. "Good to see you again."

"You as well." Tidmore straightened the hem of his tailed black jacket. "Winterly and I have sorted out the finer details surrounding our next shipment, and the accounts have arrived via messenger. All is awaiting your perusal."

"Perhaps," Winterly added, "you can peruse the correspondence after dinner, if that suits you, Ashten?"

"It certainly does." He'd complete his business this evening, then they'd be no need for him to return to Ellie's home tomorrow. Yes, he could remain safely ensconced within his own four walls with no issue, returning to his self-exile as he longed to do. Gently, he stroked Beast between the ears. "Where did you come across this pup?" he asked Winterly.

"Ellie actually found him sitting underneath one of the topiary trees in our garden last week, and yapping at the tree as if the tree were an intruder. Unfortunately, we've been unable to find who he might belong to, even sending Jeeves to knock on doors. Ellie insisted Beast would make a suitable hunting dog and I'm in agreement, so we've kept him."

"That would make this little fellow your fourth puppy?" He recalled Buster and Blue, two golden retrievers who'd always followed him and Harry about while hunting, then had come Bear, a black retriever. "Is Bear still around?"

"Yes, and in his dotage. He'll enjoy playing with this young fellow when we take Beast to Winterly Manor in the summer. Loads of wide open fields for him to bound around in."

"He'll get lost in all the tall grass if we don't keep an eye on him though," Flora warned before strolling across to Ellie.

Ellie cast her gaze to Tidmore and patted the bench beside her. "Shall we play a tune together?"

"Absolutely." Tidmore strode across to Ellie and settled on the bench seat next to her. He ran his fingers over a few keys then cleared his throat as he gazed into his Ellie's eyes.

Such delight fluttered over Ellie's face and a deep sense of unease curdled in Ashten's gut. Ellie had told him that Poole wasn't her suitor, so perhaps it was Tidmore? He gritted his teeth as Tidmore leaned in far too close to Ellie, particularly for his liking.

"What about the piece by Mozart we've been practicing?" Tidmore asked her. "Sonata for four hands in D major K. 381. If you'd like?"

"Yes, allegro first, then if you're content to continue, andante, and allegro molto to finish." Ellie glanced at her mother. "Will there be time, Mama?"

"Of course, my dear. I'll turn the pages." Flora perched on a wooden-backed chair next to the couple. "I do so enjoy the Piano Sonata, and you two play so well together."

"It's practice that perfects one's play." Ellie readied their piano music on the stand for Flora to turn.

"How long have you been playing, Tidmore?" Still gritting his teeth, Ashten forced the words out as he eased into the seat Flora had vacated. Winterly strode to the hearth and added another log to the flames.

"From my earliest years."

"Yes, Mr. Tidmore's mother is a wonderful teacher." Ellie brushed her shoulder against Tidmore's as she settled her fingers into position then she asked the well-versed man, "Are you ready?"

"Yes, on the count of three. One, two, three."

Together, Ellie and Tidmore both dropped straight into the musical beauty of the Sonata, and Ashten's heart dropped as well. Unfortunately, together, they stunned him with their passionate portrayal of Mozart's music. Clearly, they'd practiced this piece often at each other's sides and his innards twisted into a rage of knots, although even with the fierce level of tension storming through him, the playful notes of the allegro slowly wound around him, settling him just as they always did.

This piece reminded him of lighter, more fanciful times. Like before the war had ever started. Of being atop his stallion and flying across the open fields of his duchy. Then as the allegro came to an end, everyone remained quiet.

Moments later, Ellie and Tidmore dove straight into the more soulful tune of andante. With this piece of music, he returned to those grassy fields of his duchy atop his thoroughbred. He closed his eyes and drifted on the sea of melody, his Ellie playing so beautifully. He could taste the pine freshness in the air, the sunshine warming his skin, and the addictive freedom of the countryside drawing him ever deeper within it.

The puppy curled into a ball in his palms, its head and paws propped on his thumbs, then with the closing notes of the andante falling like soft rose petals fluttering to the grassy ground, he opened his eyes and caught Ellie's golden gaze as she smiled at him. "Bravo," he whispered to her, although there was still so much more to come.

She didn't disappoint either, his enchanting imp who'd followed him around since he was a lad. With her pouty lips raised and her bountiful charms on clear display, she dived straight into the allegro molto.

Her fingers chased across the keys from her position on the right, then Tidmore joined in from her left before halting and allowing Ellie to continue, then both together again. They played the piece to sheer perfection before reaching the ultimate crescendo.

He held his breath, the puppy no longer napping but his ears alert.

Ellie and Tidmore both raced to the finish line, the last chord still ringing clear about the room as she and Tidmore stood and dipped their heads to everyone's applause.

His too. He clapped with fierce abandon, the puppy yapping excitedly in his lap. He wanted to pull Ellie Marie into his arms and kiss her, to take her far away from Tidmore, who seemed incredibly pleased by their performance too, as he had every right to be.

"Oh my, nothing can surely top that performance now. You two are delightfully good together." Flora settled the music sheets into order after turning them so expertly during the playing.

"Dinner is served." A maid bobbed her head at the doorway.

"Thank you, Meg." Flora acknowledged the girl with a smile. "Let's all adjourn to the dining room."

"Allow me to escort you." Tidmore extended his arm to Ellie and she thanked him, hooked her hand around his elbow, and the two walked out.

"Are you all right, Ashten?" Winterly joined him, a speculative look in his eyes.

"Yes, of course." He tugged at the tightness of his cravat.

"Hand Beast back to Sophia. She'll put him in his basket." Winterly patted his shoulder then escorted Flora and Olivia out of the room.

He passed Sophia the pup since she stood waiting with her hands out for him, and after Sophia had snuggled the wee one in the padded basket near the fireplace, he offered Sophia his arm and escorted her down the passageway and into the dining room.

Winterly seated his mama and sister at the long table draped in a burgundy cloth, while Ashten pulled out Sophia's chair for her. Ellie sat across from her sisters, Tidmore at her side, and with Winterly and Flora now seated at each end of the table, he took the last remaining chair on Ellie's other side. Casting his gaze to Flora across the sparkling glasses and cutlery, he said, "You are all very dear to me."

"As you are very dear to us too." Flora's eyes misted and she quickly blinked. "This is a wonderful night, one to truly celebrate."

"Hear, hear," Winterly chanted before signaling the staff.

Plates were set before them. The Yorkshire pudding held a crispy baked batter shell and a light and chewy batter center, the dish served with roast beef and gravy. A generous portion of pork and apple pie sat to the side with steam curling from it, and the cubed roasted potatoes glistened with a knob of butter melting over them.

"Let's join together in a prayer of thanks." Winterly bowed his head and recited a prayer, then once done, the servants filled their wine glasses.

"Did you have success selecting your masks for the masquerade?" Ellie asked Olivia and Sophia as they ate.

"We had immense success," Olivia answered her, "Sophia and Mama found the perfect masks too."

Conversation continued to flow, while under the table, Ellie gently squeezed his leg, her bold move shocking him into momentary silence. Thank heavens none of her family had seen that.

"Look at you returning to the world." She smiled so beguilingly at him, and his heart skipped a beat.

"It's you and your family. You lot are impossible to ignore."

"I'm going to take that as a compliment." She snuck her hand back and sipped her wine as she glanced at her mama. "Ashten and I had a lovely afternoon and even played cards. I actually trounced His Grace in poker."

"Oh, I do so enjoy a game of cards. Perhaps we could all play whist after dinner?" Flora arched an expectant brow at him. "Please, say you'll stay."

"I would enjoy a game of whist immensely." He couldn't deny his desire for a chance to redeem his loss of earlier against Ellie, or at least that's what he told himself. Trounce her this time, he would, and discover if Tidmore was the man she intended to run away with while he did.

He wasn't leaving until he'd uncovered all of her secrets.

Chapter 12

At the card table set up in the drawing room, Ellie took the seat Ashten had graciously pulled out for her. Her sisters and Winterly had drawn the three smallest cards of the deck so would sit this game out and play in the second match of whist instead. Sophia and Olivia sat on the blue brocade settee fawning over Beast who kept trying to gnaw on their fingers, while Winterly poured port at the side table into glasses. Across from her, Ashten, her partner and dealer in this game as per the initial cards drawn, took his seat and handed the cards to Tidmore on his left to shuffle. Ashten accepted the cards back, asked Mama on his right to cut the deck, then dealt all the cards out, one at a time, face down, until each of them had thirteen cards, other than for him. The final card belonged to Ashten and he left it turned face up near his cards, that card being the card denoting the suit of hearts as trumps.

"This is a wonderful pairing." Mama jiggled in her seat across from Tidmore, her partner. "We shall make a winning pair, Mr. Tidmore."

"That we shall." Tidmore began the game for the first trick by leading with one of the cards in his hand, a king of diamonds.

Ellie followed suit next with her four of diamonds, then Mama added a two of the same suit and Ashten, who was last, picked the face card up and slotted it into his hand of splayed cards before playing an ace of diamonds.

"Well played." She blew Ashten a kiss, which she really shouldn't have done, and her cheeks burned with heat a mere second after the terrible gaffe.

"It appears," Mama said rather loud in order to cover her faux pas, "that Your Grace is in fine form tonight."

Oh goodness. Her cheeks heated even further. He'd been in fine form all day, in the park when they'd kissed, over dinner when he'd sat beside her, and almost every other moment in between.

"Care for some port, Ashten?" Winterly offered her card partner a glass, which he accepted with thanks, then her brother proceeded to serve everyone else in the room. As Winterly handed her a drink, he gently squeezed her shoulder and whispered in her ear, "Take care that your competitive spirit doesn't rise too sharply tonight."

"Why is that?" she whispered back. Thankfully Mama was regaling Ashten and Mr. Tidmore with an interesting tale and neither man had caught her brother's words thus far.

"Because I don't want you scaring off the two men in this house who are currently unwed and possibly looking for a wife."

"I should have known you were going to say that." Yes, there were definitely two eligible men present here tonight, but one of them had no desire to take a wife. A certainty for sure.

As their game resumed, she and Ashten took the second trick, then the third.

Mama and Tidmore claimed the fourth, fifth, and sixth tricks, and after another six heart-racing rounds with three tricks claimed to each partnered pair, it all came down to the thirteenth and final card in their hands.

"I fear I might chew my nails off." Sophia sat on the edge of the settee, eagerly watching their game.

"I've never witnessed such a close match." Olivia too was near to toppling off the seat beside Sophia.

"Neither have I." Ashten placed his card down first, an ace of hearts, a card no one could possibly beat. "Trumps," he murmured with a wicked grin at her.

"Oh my." She beamed. "Well done."

"Gads. We'll have to take the loss with good grace, Lady Winterly." Tidmore dropped his four of spades on top of Ashten's ace of hearts.

"That we will, and we were so close too." Mama placed her ten of hearts on the pile. "Show us what you had, Ellie, my dear."

"I saved my best until last." She lowered her jack of hearts on top of Mama's.

"Drat it all. You would have trumped Tidmore and me too had Ashten been without the ace." Mama rose and held out her chair for Sophia, while Tidmore held out his chair for her brother.

Ellie offered Olivia her chair for the swap then came around and touched Ashten's shoulder. "You remain and play another round since you won that last trick."

"As you wish." He collected the cards and shuffled them, while Mama sat on the settee and picked up her embroidery.

Tidmore stepped in beside her, his voice low as he murmured, "Did our plan come to fruition?"

"Yes." She cleared her throat, wishing to speak to him further in private. "I believe I need some fresh air," she said loud enough for everyone to hear.

"Then allow me to escort you for a walk." Tidmore grinned. "In the rear garden?"

"Yes, that would be lovely." She looped her arm through the crook in his elbow. "Mama?"

"I can see you from the window, dear. Go and take your walk." Mama waved her off.

"Then let's be away." She wandered into the foyer, donned her riding habit jacket hooked on the stand where Penny had hung it for her earlier, then as Mr. Tidmore opened the door, she walked through and wandered along the gravel pathway into the garden. Together, they strolled underneath the arbor, white and red rose vines clinging to it. She halted and lifted her gaze to the moon shining so gloriously bright overhead, a million stars twinkling all about it. "When I stand outside on such a beautiful, clear night as this, I can't help but wonder what it might be like to see this sky from elsewhere."

"The stars align differently depending on where one stands on this vast Earth." Tidmore clasped his hands behind his back as he gazed at the stars, then at her. The moon highlighted his strong jaw and painted the ends of his black hair a midnight blue. "If you truly do desire to see this night sky from elsewhere, I would be honored to take you to those places across the seas."

"I've always longed to travel."

"My mother would adore listening to us play the piano together, my father as well."

"When will they next return to England for a visit?"

"Usually in the summer, so they'll return soon."

"How wonderful." She smiled and snuck a look over her shoulder toward the drawing room. Mama watched them as she embroidered, her gaze dipping up and down from her stitching to the window. Ashten watched her avidly from the card table and she waved, which for some reason made him scowl. She giggled and returned her attention to Tidmore. "The duke is beginning to open his heart again, and with him being here this night and remaining for dinner and such, I'm certain he's now made that first difficult step in returning to Society, just as I wished for him to do."

"He is a very fortunate man to have such friends as you and your family, and I'm immensely glad that your brother and I have forged such a strong business partnership as well. I'm certainly looking forward to extending that partnership to the duke. With the three of us pooling our abilities and funds together, we can expand the shipping fleet I manage, just as I've always desired to do." He cleared his throat. "Tell me about the finer details surrounding your conversation with the duke."

"In the end, I was forced to carry out the plan we hatched."

"I expected that was so." A slow nod.

"You don't mind that I did?" She lowered her voice further, even though she didn't need to. They were alone, their conversation private.

"Of course not. I would never have suggested the elopement as an idea otherwise."

"Ashten still believes I intend on eloping, but I never disclosed with whom, so you are safe in that regard."

"In all honesty, I've no issue with Ashten learning it is me."

"Pardon?" Her breath hitched.

"What I'm trying to say, is that I believe your brother would approve of a marriage between us, even if it came by way of an elopement. Before dinner this evening, he spoke about his worry regarding Sophia, of Hargrove's decision to join the hussars, which surprised me since it is of such a deeply personal nature."

"Winterly would only ever speak of such private family matters with those he holds in great esteem."

"I would never disclose to another what he spoke of to me, other than with you of course." He reached for a rose dangling from the arbor overtop her head and plucked it free. The white petals glowed an enchanting shade of gold in the moonlight. "You and I have always been rather candid with each other, which is rather refreshing compared to my conversations with so many of the debutantes of London. You must also wed soon yourself, from what I understand from your brother, and even though we spoke of an elopement in order to draw the Duke of Ashten out of Blackgale House, I would love nothing more than for you to agree to an elopement in truth."

"You would?" Her mouth dried completely out.

"Yes, I most certainly would." He laid the rose gently in his palm and held it out to her, his gaze firm on hers. "Lady Ellie Trentbury, would you care to travel the world with me, to the Americas and beyond when I'm on board one of my ships? I can promise you we'll live here in England half the year. I would be greatly honored if you would agree to be my wife."

"Y-you're—" She was lost for words. Never had she envisioned actually eloping with Tidmore, although if she did elope with him to Gretna Green, then Sophia could accept a proposal from Hargrove should he request her hand in marriage before he left for the front line. Goodness. Tidmore was certainly suitable, and she'd always enjoyed his company. They had a great deal in common, and he and her brother got along so very well. Mama also approved of him, and Ashten, well, he'd stated his intentions well and clear. There would never be a marriage between them. She drew in a deep, fortifying breath. "You have an immensely generous and giving heart, Mr. Tidmore."

"Call me Thomas, and is that yes, Lady Ellie?"

"You must call me Ellie, and..." She touched the rose in Thomas's hand and gently brushed one finger over a soft petal, her gaze on his. He had such kind eyes, a soft brown that emitted compassion, and so much more. "I, ah, I would need to warn you first, of my head strong and frivolous nature."

"Then I need to warn you as well. I have had no issue in the past telling a lady with golden eyes that she can elope with me, so that the duke she wished to aid might tear himself out of his self-exile and rejoin Society." He searched her gaze. "I can see you hold Ashten in high regard, and one day I hope you shall also hold me in equally high regard."

"I'm certain I already do."

"Then, my dear Lady Ellie, if you care to elope with me in truth, we shall do so the night of the masquerade, while the ball is in full swing and no one will miss our departure. Just be sure to leave a note behind for your brother so he won't worry over where you've gone. Inform him that I shall take immense care of you, and that we shall return from Gretna Green once we've spoken our vows." He held the rose by the stem toward her. "Will you accept this rose as a token of my affection?"

"Yes." She could do naught less.

Chapter 13

Deep in Ashten's gut, turmoil raged. He'd barely been able to sit still as he'd played cards, not while outside under the arbor abloom with white and red roses, his Ellie was conducting a rather intimate conversation with Mr. Tidmore. Damn the man. Unfortunately, he actually liked and respected the American shipping merchant. He was clearly an honorable man with a sound business mind, a partner Winterly had forged a close business relationship with, and a man he intended on fostering the same business relationship with too, but hell, he truly didn't care for how close those two stood together under the moonlight.

Obviously, he was jealous. Even he could admit that annoying emotion had risen strongly within him, but she wasn't for him, could never be for him. Not only was she Harry's little sister, but he'd sworn off getting involved with any and all ladies after what had happened to Lady Ashley.

Gritting his teeth, he played his next card and dash it all, Ellie had just accepted a rose from Tidmore. She brought the white bloom to her nose, snuck a look at him through the window and suddenly frowned. Worry creased her brow, her pouty lips forming the words, *Are you all right?*

Of course he wasn't all right, and he wouldn't be either until she returned to the drawing room and removed herself from the private conversation she was currently having outside. Good grief. The man held such a damn besotted look on his face as he gazed upon his Ellie. His Ellie. He mouthed back to her, *No*.

Ellie nodded then hooked one arm through Tidmore's and steered the man back along the gravel pathway to the front door. Moments later, the door creaked open and clicked shut. Ellie's giggle filtered through from the foyer then she and Tidmore swept into the room, the man with a wide smile on his face and clear adoration twinkling in his eyes. Not good. Not good at all.

"It's your turn, Ashten." Olivia glanced from him to Ellie then back to him. "You'll need the ace of spades to beat Winterly's king of spades, otherwise you and I are sunk."

"My apologies," he murmured to Olivia. "I've gotten a little distracted during our game, and my last card is a ten." He played his ten of spades, which wasn't nearly high enough even though in the suit of trumps.

"We did our best, Your Grace." Olivia swatted Winterly's arm as he grinned madly. "You're gloating."

"I didn't even say a word."

"You're still gloating."

Sophia laughed, her grin just as gloating as Winterly's.

"You two are impossible." Olivia cast her gaze to Flora. "Mama, you should be telling them both off."

"I would, my dear, but you've already done so, and rather well at that."

"Congratulations, Winterly, Sophia. A game well played and won." Ashten straightened in his chair as Ellie left Tidmore's side and settled a hand on his shoulder from behind. Her touch instantly soothed him, and luckily her family didn't raise any eyebrows. Still, it took all his willpower not to lift his hand and cover hers on his shoulder in return, then to tug her around and settle her in his lap. That certainly wouldn't go down well, would most certainly end in Winterly demanding suitable recompense for his behavior. Possibly in the way of a marriage proposal. Hmm, temptation stirred in his chest, the enticement almost too much to bear. His fingers tingled to make a grab for her.

"Mama, come and play." Winterly stood and tapped his chair for her. "I'd like to adjourn to my study with Ashten and Tidmore. You four ladies can play another game together while we complete our business for the night."

"I'd love to play another game." Flora set her embroidery aside and took Winterly's chair.

Ashten offered his chair to Ellie and tucked it in after she sat.

Desperately, he wished to dunk his nose in her hair and get another deep inhale of her beguiling scent, that of sunshine and fresh air, laughter and love. Those aromas clung to her, and he wanted more of it. Instead, he stepped back from her and smiled at Flora. "In case you're all abed when our business concludes, I'd like to thank you now for the wonderful meal and your family's delightful company this night."

"You are most welcome. It's wonderful having you here, quite akin in fact to having Harry home. There's a sense of my family being complete, if you understand what I mean."

"I do, and you honor me with such a comparison." He kissed Flora's knuckles, then kissed Olivia's. "When we partner again for another game, I shall do my best not to let you down a second time."

"I'm going to hold you to that promise." Olivia gave him a stern look as he released her fingers, one which made him chuckle. She was so like Ellie in nature.

He brushed a kiss across Sophia's knuckles then returned to Ellie's side, his thoughts all askew. He frowned as he held her hand and brought her fingers to his lips. "Thank you for the lovely day."

"Even though I trounced you in poker?"

"Even so. I thoroughly enjoyed myself at the park." He released her hand before he no longer could then joined Winterly and Tidmore at the door. He followed the men into Winterly's study and eased into one of the two forest-green corner padded chairs sitting either side of the lit fireplace, while Tidmore took the other.

Winterly stood at his chunky oak desk and riffled through a stack of investment reports, then after finding what he was after, handed him several pages. "These are the accounts which cover the past year's profits we've made. With your financial contribution though, we won't just double that number this coming year, but quadruple it."

He studied the pages, giving his full attention to the figures listed. Winterly and Tidmore answered his questions and together they discussed the finer details surrounding their charges for carrying goods, their intended diversification and cargo. Indeed, if he added the same amount of funds to their investment which both Tidmore and Winterly had already done, then they could easily quadruple any profit made. With a smile, he eyed both men and gave them his answer. "I'm on board."

"You won't regret this partnership, Ashten." Winterly shook his hand.

"I second that." Tidmore shook his hand too, while Winterly poured brandy from a decanter into three glasses and handed them each a glass.

They toasted their coming venture together, and Ashten settled back into his chair as Tidmore recounted his exploits to date. From the man's tales, he wasn't just honorable, but a true gentleman in that he considered his crew's needs just as strongly as he considered his own, and that sat rather well with Ashten. It was no wonder Winterly and Ellie both enjoyed Tidmore's company.

Hours later, the logs in the fire mere embers, he rose to his feet. "I'll hand these papers to my man-of-affairs in the morning, and ensure the funds you need are sent through as quickly as possible."

"Excellent." Tidmore dipped his head to him. "If you need any further documents, don't hesitate to ask and I'll send whatever you need directly to you."

"I shall."

"It's been a rather eventful evening, gentlemen, one I've thoroughly enjoyed." Winterly walked him and Tidmore to the front door.

All remained quiet farther along the passageway, the drawing room dark, although candles glowed within the iron wall sconces along the stairwell and across the top landing. It had to be well after midnight, the ladies all abed.

Tidmore strode down the front steps and gestured for the stable hand to ready his horse and once the lad brought his mount forward into the driveway, Tidmore swung into the saddle and with a wave to him and Winterly, trotted down the moonlit street.

Ashten rubbed his achy leg. Sitting for hours on end usually caused it to stiffen and he leaned more heavily against his cane as he lifted his greatcoat from the coat rack.

"Stretch and loosen your leg if you need to," Winterly offered. "Then see yourself out when you're ready. Jeeves will ensure the door is locked when he extinguishes the candles."

"I'd appreciate that before I mount up."

"Have a good night then, Ashten." Winterly strode up the stairs and disappeared into the darkness.

He massaged his leg then using the wall at his back, braced himself against it and lowered into a squat before rising again. Another two squats and his muscles started to stretch and relax.

"Ashten?" Ellie's whisper came from somewhere along the upper landing, then she snuck downstairs in a white robe, the hem swishing across her bare toes. With her golden locks free and swaying down her back, she ducked into the dark confines of the drawing room, snuck her head back out and glared at him. "Hurry up. I need to talk to you before you leave, and I don't want Winterly or Jeeves seeing us together."

"You're asking for trouble, Ellie." He should ignore her request and walk out the front door, only he couldn't stop himself from striding into the darkened drawing room after her and searching the shadows. "Where are you?"

"Here." She caught his hand and tugged him behind the door, her breath coming hard and fast, just as his did.

"What did you want to talk about?" He kept his voice low, a mere whisper as he fumbled to find her in the dark. He did though, and curled his hands around her soft cheeks.

"I need to know if your position has changed since your last declaration."

"Which position and which declaration would that have been?"

"You said you'd thoroughly enjoyed yourself at the park."

"I wouldn't have stated so otherwise."

"That's not exactly what I'm asking." She huffed under her breath, and he damn well wished he could see the frustration which must be passing across her face.

Gently, he traced his fingers down her cheeks and along her lips, beautifully plump and kissable lips. "What are you asking, my sweet?"

"I suppose I'm asking what type of spring flower would you choose should you happen upon a garden abloom with flowers? A fragrant rose, an elegant lily, or would you still choose nothing at all?"

"That is a strange question."

"Just answer it." Another huffing breath.

"I'm particularly fond of daisies."

"Daisies? But they grow wild everywhere."

"Which is exactly why I'm so very fond of them. The sight of them brings back such wonderful memories, particularly of my childhood. Do you remember the daisy chains you used to weave together then hang all about Winterly Manor? They popped up all about the place, hanging from the banister, the chandeliers, as well as draped over the back of a chair or two."

"I'm not sure you quite understand my question. Come with me." She snuck out of the drawing room, tiptoed across to a flower arrangement gracing the foyer table and plucked a daisy free then offered it to him. "Would you accept this daisy, Pierce?"

"I have no need for a daisy right now."

"Yes, which is as you've said all along. You would still choose nothing, or I should say no one, at all." She dropped the daisy on the table then backed away toward the stairs. "I wish you a good night, and may tomorrow bring you what you most desire."

"Wait." He snagged her hand before she could escape. "Where are you going?"

"Back to bed."

"Before you do, and since we're chatting so openly, I have a question for you. Is Tidmore the one you intend on eloping with?"

"That question I can't answer."

"You two seem rather close."

"I haven't kissed him if that's what you're asking." She grasped his lapels and reached up on her toes. "Don't ever give up on life again. Instead, grab ahold of it by both hands and never let it go. You must live. Promise me you will."

"It sounds suspiciously as if you're wishing me a fond farewell."

"I am, for you are fond of daisies, but don't intend on ever taking one." She brushed a kiss across his cheek. "Good night, Your Grace. Sleep well."

He let her slip away from him, the candlelight shimmering across her freckled cheeks as she dashed back upstairs, then when she reached the top landing, she blew him a kiss and his heart clenched in on itself.

Chapter 14

Early the next evening, right on sunset and after readying herself for her coming night with Tidmore at one of the playhouses on Drury Lane, Ellie halted at Sophia's doorway. Soft murmurs echoed from within, both Sophia and Olivia's. She touched the not-quite-closed door, pushed it open, and ducked her head in. Sophia sat on the floral-padded armchair before the window in a pretty lavender day dress with lace edging the heart-shaped neckline, her golden locks falling in soft curls down her back and her gaze fixed on the rear garden beyond the topiary trees, while Olivia sat on the end of Sophia's canopied bed. "My dear sisters, I missed the request for a meeting."

"There is no meeting, just interesting conversation." Sophia turned from the window with a soft smile. "Mr. Tidmore has arrived with Lord and Lady Marriweather in their carriage, and you look glorious in your evening gown. I do adore it when you wear ivory satin and lace."

"I do too." Olivia patted the red-gold bedcovers beside her. "The combination and color suits your complexion to perfection."

"Thank you." She eased down on the bed and clasped Olivia's hand in hers. "What have you both been discussing?"

"Actually, you." Olivia squeezed her fingers. "We're worried."

"About what exactly?" She and her sisters never kept any secrets from each other.

"We're wondering about you and Tidmore." Leaning forward in her chair, Sophia tapped the armrest. "The two of you had quite an intense conversation in the garden last night, yet when you returned, you swept right in behind Ashten and comforted him with a hand on his shoulder. He wasn't at all relaxed until you returned, his attention consumed by both you and Tidmore outside and not on the game we played."

"You don't look at Tidmore the same way you look at Ashten." Olivia squeezed her fingers. "That's impossible to miss."

"I could sense Ashten needed comforting when I returned, and why the comparison to Tidmore?"

"You told us Tidmore proposed, so of course we're making the comparison." A huff from Sophia as she left her chair and sat on her other side. "Do you intend on eloping with him?"

"I must marry."

"There's always been a special bond between you and Ashten, right from a very young age." Olivia frowned as she spoke. "You alone were the one who dragged him out of Blackgale House when no one else could."

"Yes, but he came here yesterday because of Winterly's missive," she countered.

"Humbug."

"Don't humbug me." She tsked Olivia under her breath. "I'm telling the truth."

"No matter whether Winterly had invited him to attend a business meeting here with himself and Mr. Tidmore, I'm certain Ashten came because he wished to see you." Olivia raised a challenging brow. "Why else did he race after you and Poole not half an hour after you'd left? Winterly told us so when we quizzed him about what had happened on our return from town, and dare I say it, but both Sophia and I believe Ashten took off after you because his jealousy arose, and a man doesn't get jealous unless he cares."

"If there's any jealousy on Ashten's part, he won't do anything about it. Ashten has even declined the chance of taking me to wife." Heat flushed her cheeks, but she didn't lower her gaze, only held her position with her sisters. "He doesn't wish for anything more than mere friendship with me, and there's also the fact that I've turned down five proposals and both of you will one day wish to wed. I must accept a betrothal at some point, so why not with Tidmore? He's so very similar to me in nature, and we have the same interests too, the piano and the desire to seek adventures on the high seas. I could come to love him, given time."

Sophia knelt at her feet and grasped her hand. "Ellie, please, if you're agreeing to elope because of me and Olivia, then don't. Between the three of us we can find a way to get around Winterly, and Hargrove hasn't proposed to me as yet. Maybe he will, and maybe he won't. He only speaks of joining the hussars and his duty to fight in this war. I can't halt him in his duty, nor do I wish to."

"I agree with Sophia. Don't do anything rash." Olivia squeezed her hands, tears swimming in her eyes, just as they swam in Sophia's.

"I hate that we must choose to either wed or become spinsters." Sophia lowered her forehead to Ellie's lap. "I love you both so much."

"I love you both too." Hot tears burned in Ellie's eyes. "And no matter what decision I make, I will forever hold you both in my heart. We will always be sisters." She hugged them both tight, then wiped her tears from her cheeks and once she'd composed herself again, she brushed the wrinkles from her ivory gown, tugged on her gloves and adjusted the fur-lined cloak she'd already secured at her neck. "I must go, otherwise Winterly will check on me and discover us all crying. That will only upset him."

Her sisters nodded their agreement and she left.

She walked downstairs, pushed a smile on her face and entered the drawing room and then smiled in truth. Lord Marriweather stood with Tidmore and Winterly next to the fireplace, the men with whisky glasses in hand, her brother leaning one arm on the oak mantel and their conversation on shipping, cargo, and such. Yes, Tidmore got on famously well with her brother. He would do very well as a husband, and as Tidmore caught sight of her, he set his whisky glass on the side table next to the decanter and crossed to her.

He bowed, his white cravat knotted and his black tailcoats swaying, his navy breeches tight-fitting and his mid-calf Hessian boots bearing an up-peaking front with a golden tassel gleaming from the top lip. "You look radiant," he murmured as he caught her hand and kissed her fingers. "I've been looking forward to this evening since we parted company last night. The hours in between have rambled on endlessly until now."

"You flatter me far too much." Such endearing words, and she adored him for issuing them.

"Yes, you indeed look radiant, my dear." Mama rose from the blue brocade settee next to Matilde, her second cousin who'd wed Marriweather two years past. Mama gave Tidmore a delightful smile, her voice pitched almost girlishly high as she continued, "Ellie's papa said the same thing to me the very night before he lowered to one knee and—"

"Mama!" She struck a shocked and hopefully pointed look that said, *Don't say another word.*

"—proposed." Mama grinned mischievously then caught her hand and drew her toward Matilde. "Ellie, Matilde is here and has just shared some wonderful news with us all tonight. Your cousin and her husband are expecting their first child together in the early autumn. Isn't that wonderful?"

"Oh yes, indeed that's wonderful. You have my heartfelt

congratulations." She grasped Matilde's hands as her cousin stood, then hugged her and kissed her cheeks, first her left then her right. Excitement for Matilde thrummed through her. "How have you been feeling?"

"I'm afraid morning sickness has kept me abed for several weeks, but now I'm finally past that dreadful stage, I couldn't be happier." Her cousin's cheeks glowed a rosy hue, the same color as her evening gown, her dark hair pinned atop her head with artful curls escaping.

"I should have paid a visit." It had been far too long since they'd last caught up.

"We've remained in the country while I've been unwell so you wouldn't have been able to."

"Is morning sickness truly dreadful?" Her cousin would be honest with her.

"It is when that sickness isn't confined only to the mornings." Matilde blew out a long breath which fluttered her curls. "It should in fact be called all-day sickness."

"Yes, I agree," Mama added. "My own morning sickness with each of my five children was tediously difficult and unfortunately there's no solution to the illness other than for those early months to pass and for the babe to grow. Once all settles down, so does the sickness."

"My babe certainly grows." Lovingly, Matilde stroked her belly.

"May I?" Ellie held out a hand, her excitement growing.

"Of course, you may." Brimming with pleasure, her cousin caught both her hands and brought them softly to rest on her small bump. "It truly is a miracle to be with child. I had begun to fear naught would happen since our second wedding anniversary came and passed with still no child to speak of."

"My mother feared the same after four years of marriage with my father." Tidmore uttered the words from Ellie's side, having joined her. "Yet she gave birth to my eldest brother the following year, then I arrived soon after, followed by my three sisters."

"Yes, sometimes it can simply take a little time for a babe to come." Mama popped a kiss on Matilde's cheek. "You wouldn't want to miss the opening scene of the play, so the four of you should be away."

"Yes, we should, and this will be my first play in quite some time. I'm looking forward to it." Matilde collected her rose silk reticule from the settee then linked arms with Ellie and they followed the men into the foyer where they collected their greatcoats and hats.

Winterly opened the front door for them, even though the footman stood waiting, then beamed as she passed him by. "Have an enjoyable night out, dear sister."

"I'm sure I shall."

Together, the four of them walked down the driveway and stepped into the awaiting Marriweather coach and she sat beside her cousin on the rear padded seat, while Tidmore and Marriweather eased onto the front seat. The viscount tapped the roof with his cane and called out to his driver, "To Drury Lane."

The slap of the reins resounded and they jerked forward, the horses soon settling into a smooth gait as they traveled the streets toward the West End playhouses. The skies darkened further and the moon rose with a blaze of stars sprinkled all about.

Once they arrived at the playhouse farther down the street from where another theater was being rebuilt after a terrible fire, they alighted out. The usual busyness of the carpenters hard at work during the daytime hours had ceased, the ricocheting blows of their hammers now quiet, and the only noise that of the excited *ton* who'd arrived in their carriages to enjoy a night out just as they had.

After walking inside the grand entranceway, Ellie made her way to Marriweather's box on the fourth floor, her cousin and the viscount taking two of the four burgundy padded chairs along the front row.

Tidmore, his hand resting gently over hers tucked into the crook of his arm, bent his head to hers near the rear curtains in the dark where they couldn't be seen. "Marriweather also invited another gentleman here tonight, as well as his plus one, and before they arrive I thought it best to warn you of who that gentleman will be."

"If you need to warn me, then it must be Marriweather's younger brother." She looked into the deep brown depths of his eyes. "His brother is quite the scoundrel, but still rather loveable all the same."

"No, it's not his brother who'll be joining us, but instead Captain Poole."

"Oh, how interesting." Surprise certainly took her.

"My thoughts exactly."

"I haven't heard from Poole today." She'd been expecting a note to arrive at the very least, perhaps even flowers to accompany his words of regret at having to leave her behind in the park.

"Poole requested the invitation after you accepted my offer to come," Tidmore told her. "Are you interested in the man at all?"

"No, and I only accepted a ride with Poole in the park in order to distract Ashten from learning exactly who my supposed suitor was." An honest answer, one the man she'd agreed to elope with deserved to know.

"Then if we are to be away to Gretna Green tomorrow night, I need you to take all care around the captain."

"Of course."

"Thank you for understanding my request." He gestured for her to take a seat beside her cousin and she sat while he eased into the chair next to hers.

Heavy burgundy curtains hid the stage from view, denying them anything of interest as yet to watch, so she removed her dainty opera glasses from her reticule, just as Matilde had done and trained them on the audience. This booth held a prime position at the front of the house, with a bird's eye view of both the players once they stepped onto the stage, and the other patrons who'd chosen to sit in the main auditorium below. She could even see across to the booths on the other side with no issue, the chandeliers above alight with candles.

She cast her gaze along the boxes next to them and halted when she caught sight of the shadowed form of someone standing in the very rear of the Duke of Ashten's box. Ashten hadn't attended a play since his return from the war and as the curtains shifted and the shadowed form disappeared, she clapped a hand over her mouth. Perhaps it had simply been one of playhouse's staff ensuring all was clear in his box, or perhaps a cleaning maid. No one else other than those who paid for these boxes were permitted entry within them and constant checks were made.

"Good evening, everyone." Captain Poole entered with a flourish, his fine jacket buttoned and a young lady at his side. "Meet Miss Sarah Shepherd, my brother's betrothed."

"Good evening, Miss Shepherd." Marriweather crossed to the couple. "Welcome and do take a seat. The play has yet to begin."

"Thank you." Miss Shepherd accepted Poole's escort to her seat, the young lady wearing a pearl-colored evening gown with thick petticoats under her full skirts, her lacy kid gloves fitting snuggly all the way to her elbows and flowers adorning the wide brim of her hat. Behind Miss Shepherd, her maid stepped into the booth and settled herself on a stool at the rear.

"It's wonderful to meet you." Ellie smiled warmly at the young lady. "Captain Poole told me how you and your betrothed met. Are you enjoying your time in town?"

"Yes, immensely, and it's wonderful spending time with my betrothed's family." A flutter of her fan.

Poole clapped Tidmore on the back. "A fine night it is to be out and enjoying oneself."

"Yes, it surely is," Tidmore answered him with a slight shift of his shoulders.

"Did all go well on your return to the War Office?" she questioned Poole, not wishing to ignore what had happened in the park with his urgent leaving.

"All was cleared up and is now most certainly well." Poole glanced at Miss Shepherd. "I was with Lady Ellie and the Duke of Ashten in Hyde Park when I received a message from Bishophale to attend him at the Horse Guards in Whitehall." He cast his gaze back to Ellie. "Speaking of the duke, I'm rather glad he was with us at the time. I truly hated leaving you as directly as I did. Did the two of you have a pleasant afternoon?"

"Yes, we finished off your glorious Spanish wine and played cards."

A trumpet blasted and the playhouse's presenter, in his tailed coat and stiff white shirt, stepped onto the stage from between the burgundy curtains and bowed. Eloquently, he welcomed them all, then spoke of the play to be shown, the play titled Othello, as well as the cast to whom would be serving them with their night's entertainment, then he stepped aside with another deep bow and a flourishing wave of his hand as the curtain swished open.

Act one began with Roderigo taking center stage, the actor portraying a rich and self-indulgent gentleman who complained without halt to his friend Iago. A secret marriage had occurred between Desdemona and Othello, and Desdemona, being the daughter of a senator, had gone ahead and wed a Moorish general in the Venetian army. Roderigo was terribly upset. He loved Desdemona and had already asked her father for her hand in marriage and Iago listened on, the actor's cunning performance bone-chilling.

Desdemona was an ethereal vision in a white and silver

gown, her hair the same soft white shade as her dress with long locks rippling down her back, and Ellie couldn't help but admire the actress's wonderful interpretation of Desdemona. She played her part to perfection. Certainly, she'd never seen this actress on this stage before and she picked up the program handed to her upon her entry and scanned the names. Next to Desdemona's name the space had been left blank, so perhaps the actress was a stand-in who'd accepted the role at the last minute, but by goodness, she was exquisite in how she moved about the stage, as if she owned the floor.

After the first intermission had passed and the second act begun, Ellie was no closer to learning who the actress could be, and the auditorium was abuzz with wonder, just as she was.

Throughout each act that followed, Desdemona floated in a dance, each move executed with stunning fluidity and the elegance born of a lady of the peerage.

"Someone must know who she is," Matilde whispered in her ear as she peered through her theater glasses to get a better look at the actress.

"I would dearly love to know." The final moments of the last scene played out, Desdemona's death by strangulation at Othello's hands—in their bedchamber no less—and all because Othello had believed his wife guilty of adultery.

More death ensued as the truth became clear.

Treachery from Iago.

Desdemona had been innocent.

Othello slashed at Iago, not quite killing him before taking his own life in great despair of what he'd done by killing his wife.

The curtains swished across and applause resounded about the house.

What a magnificent performance.

Ellie clapped and waited anxiously for the curtains to reopen.

They did and Othello rose from the floor, held out his hand to Desdemona lying prone on the bed, her face powdered and her wig hiding her identity, which appeared wouldn't be discovered this night.

The cast joined together in the center of the stage and bowed, then the curtains swished across a second time, taking them swiftly from her sight and that of the house.

"I've never seen her before, but her performance was exquisite." Poole leaned forward from his seat behind them. "Miss Shepherd and I were actually in the foyer during the last intermission when we caught word that she might be the daughter of one of the peerage, which could be why her name is missing from the program."

"Oh, we must discover if that is true." Matilde's eyes went wide.

"No, we certainly won't." Marriweather patted his wife's hand, the affection in his gaze clear to see. "We'd be a bloodthirsty lot if we wished to expose Desdemona's true identity when she's clearly chosen to keep it a secret. It wouldn't be right."

"Oh, yes, you're right, although annoyingly so." Matilde frowned at her husband. "Alas, now, I will always be in wonder of who she might be."

"So will I." Poole stood and offered Miss Shepherd his hand. "Allow me to escort you downstairs for some refreshments." To Marriweather, he smiled and said, "You have my thanks for allowing us to join you this evening."

"Anytime, old chap, anytime."

Chapter 15

Ashten remained hidden deep within the shadows at the rear of his box throughout the whole performance of Othello. It had taken all his willpower to remain quiet and still while Tidmore and Poole remained so close to Ellie in Marriweather's booth, but as soon as the performance came to an end, he slipped behind the curtains and waited for her and the Marriweathers to leave the playhouse and step into their carriage.

As soon as they did, he mounted his stallion and rode hard to Ellie's home, beating the carriage's route easily. Hidden atop his horse behind thick bushes near her driveway, he lifted a hand to acknowledge his footman, Watts, who'd remained out of sight keeping a watchful eye on Ellie since he'd left her the night before.

Unease had eaten away at him when he'd returned home to his manor on Park Lane, and when he'd walked through the front door of Blackgale House and stood in his front foyer, he'd groaned at the silence. Within Ellie's home immense love and lively conversation rebounded off every wall. Even their puppy yapped and played wherever the wee thing wished. Within his home, everything was in order, without a speck of dust about, or an ornament sitting where it shouldn't. Flowers bloomed in a vase on the side table, all beautiful and displaying an array of vivid springtime blooms, yet not one daisy graced the damned perfect bunch.

He wanted a daisy, and this morning when he'd awoken it had been with renewed energy.

He was tired of being enclosed within the parameters he'd set for himself following the death of Lady Ashley. Ellie was right. Ashley would never have agreed to his proposal, not when she'd already chosen another man. Now, the only woman he wanted to take to wife was his best friend's little sister, which meant he needed to do some serious groveling and apologizing if he wished to see that happen. He certainly couldn't allow Ellie to make such a terrible mistake and run away with another man, unless of course that man was him.

Hooves clopped and Marriweather's carriage slowly rolled to a stop in Ellie's driveway.

Tidmore aided Ellie from the carriage and walked her to her front door. She searched her reticule, possibly for the house key to let herself in since she hadn't knocked on the door and awoken one of the staff to allow her entry. Blast it all. Winterly or Jeeves should be up waiting for her, to ensure she safely made it inside.

"Ellie?" Tidmore's voice traveled to him, the man still standing at Ellie's back.

"Yes, Thomas." Ellie turned and smiled at his new business partner. Hell and damnation, she'd spoken the man's first name.

"At the masquerade tomorrow night, I shall send a footman with a missive to you." He lifted her gloved hand to his lips and dropped a kiss on her knuckles. "Once you receive that missive, follow the instructions."

"Of course."

Double hell and damnation. It was Tidmore she intended on eloping with and tomorrow night no less. That wasn't happening, not on his watch.

"Good night, and sleep well." Tidmore leaned in and tried to brush a kiss across Ellie's cheek, although she stepped back a touch before he succeeded.

"Good night to you too."

"All will be well tomorrow evening. I'll make certain of it." Tidmore gave her a reassuring smile then strode back with a lively step to the waiting carriage.

Ellie waved to the departing coach then sagged against the door. His horse snorted, and she straightened and peered directly toward the bush he hid behind, although thankfully he remained shrouded in darkness. With a shake of her head, she found her key and slipped inside, and the moment she did, he bounded from his stallion, tethered it to a branch and gestured for Watts to keep an eye on his prized possession then using the shadows, he snuck around the side of the house without detection and glared at Ellie's bedchamber window on the second-floor above. The gentle glow of a candle lit the closed lilac drapes, then a few minutes later the light was extinguished and the glow dispersed.

He propped his cane against the side of the house and gripped the exterior.

Time to make his move.

Chapter 16

Tucked underneath her quilted lilac bedcovers, Ellie drifted toward sleep. A creak, then a soft rustle. Her drapes swayed in the nighttime breeze. Oh dear, Penny must have left her window open. She eased out of bed, tiptoed across the white woolen mat, her cream nightgown brushing her ankles. A shadowed figure slipped through the gap in the drapes and she opened her mouth to scream, but got slapped across the mouth with a hand.

"Shh, it's just me." A ragged whisper.

"Ashten?"

"Yes, who else did you expect to have sneaking into your bedchamber at such a late hour?" He released her, swept past and bolted the door then dropped his greatcoat onto the corner padded armchair and crossed his arms before her. "Clearly, we need to speak, and it can't wait."

"At this time of the night?"

"This is the only time we have left since you clearly intend on running away tomorrow night." He lit the candle on her bedside table next to a glass bowl filled with water and floating daisies. He stared at those daisies, the gentle glow of the candle illuminating the rugged lines of his face and the fierce determination now etched into his handsome features.

"You're in my bedchamber." She thumped her hands on her hips, her hair loose and swaying down her back. "Have you gone mad?"

"Tit for tat, my sweet."

"This is not the same as when I visited you in your chamber. For starters, you were fully dressed, and it wasn't the middle of the night. I came through your front door, not scaled the side of your house like a thief."

"I'm currently dressed, so that remains the same." He motioned to his beige trousers and white linen shirt underneath his superfine beige jacket, his white cravat knotted at his neck.

"But I'm not dressed if you haven't noticed." She gave him a purposeful stare.

"I can only see your toes poking out from under your nightgown. You're as fully dressed as you need to be." He swept his gaze over her chest, his lips slowly lifting. "Well, perhaps there's a nipple or two doing some poking as well. Are you cold? Do you need a blanket?"

"Cease looking at my—my—" She crossed her arms over her breasts since her nipples were indeed poking through the thin cotton. "You have clearly gone mad."

"Yes, I'm mad with lust and there's only one woman who can satisfy that lust and cure me of the desperation I currently feel." He reached out and gently caught her cheeks in his hands, his voice lowering to a husky growl as he continued, "That woman would be you, in case I hadn't quite made that clear."

"You certainly made that clear by climbing through my window, which by way, how did you manage to do with your bad leg?"

"Bad leg or not, I'm a hussar and we're trained to navigate all sorts of difficult terrain." He stroked his fingers back and forth across her cheeks. "Climbing in here wasn't an issue. My injured leg even cooperated with my need to get to you as quickly as possible."

"You said we needed to speak."

"I don't want you seeing Tidmore anymore, or Poole for

that matter."

"You have no right to tell me who I may or may not see."

"Promise me that you won't run away with Tidmore tomorrow night."

"I said—"

He let out a fierce growl then dipped his head and captured her mouth with his. Their mouths molded together, his passion erupting and she could barely hold onto her own passion as he devoured her mouth.

It was the headiest, roughest and most sensual kiss of her life, his tongue sweeping over hers as he drugged her. In a frenzy, she gripped the front of his jacket and tore it open. The buttons popped off and pinged against the walls as they scattered about her room. She desperately needed this moment with him and even though she'd been shocked at his abrupt arrival, now all she wanted to do was take advantage of it. "Pierce," she whispered against his lips. "Don't stop kissing me."

"I need you." Tension vibrated in his voice. "Tell me you need me as well."

"I do need you." She always had.

"I want you to touch me, as freely as you might wish to." He pushed his jacket from his shoulders, unknotted his cravat then dived back in and kissed her again.

She spread her hands over his wide chest and worked the buttons of his shirt open then pushed the linen aside. What a wickedly muscled chest. "I can't believe I'm actually touching you."

"All I ask is that you don't stop."

Intoxicated, she slowly trailed one finger between the rigid indents of his abs. She swished along the waistband of his trousers, her heart hammering so loud it pounded in her ears. "We shouldn't be doing this."

"Give me this moment, Ellie." His breath, all sultry and hot, fanned across her cheeks.

"Why are you here?"

"I don't want any other man touching you." He tugged the front lacings of her nightgown free, slipped the loose neckline over one shoulder and lowered his head to her breast as he freed it. His hot mouth fastened over her beaded nipple and such a fierce explosion of sensation rippled through her.

She clutched his shoulders and held on as her world tilted. "Pierce?"

"I've got you." He scooped her into his arms before she toppled, laid her gently on her bed then slid in overtop of her. He suctioned his mouth over her nipple once more and flicked the tip with his tongue. "Your breasts are so beautiful, so full and delicious."

He pushed her nightgown down to her waist and cool air flowed over her other breast. He latched onto her other nipple and gave it the same dedicated attention as he'd given the first, then he rumbled against her skin, "I need to touch more of you, Ellie. Say yes."

"Yes." The word slipped out before she could halt it.

"This might shock you, where I want to touch you that is." He lifted the skirts of her nightgown, delved underneath the cream cotton and cupped her mound with his palm. "I'm going to touch inside of you."

"Why?"

"Because touching you there will bring us both pleasure."

"How can that be?"

"Let me show you." A wicked grin and he nipped her lips then kissed her deeply and passionately. As he did, he moved his hand over her below, one finger gliding along her entrance.

Craving more but not sure what, she allowed her instincts their release and arched her back, her breasts pushing into his chest and her nipples stiffening even further as they brushed across his bare skin. "This feels magical."

"There's more to come yet." He thumbed her nub, the area

so sensitive and she arched her back, almost lurched off the bed.

"That's it, my sweet. Give me all of you." He stroked her more firmly, so expertly and she got slicker and hotter.

She ached for him deep inside. "I—I—Pierce, I'm not sure what I need."

"It's all right. I know what you need."

He pushed one finger deep inside her channel, applied more pressure to her nub then flicked his finger against it. Raw, naked need blazed through her and just as she opened her mouth, he kissed her again and muffled her cry.

Sweet pleasure speared through her, so swift and fast, then she floated somewhere far away from her body. Dreamily, she finally came back down and when she did, she smiled at the man gazing deep into her eyes and murmured, "That was beautiful, but you didn't put yourself inside of me, and you said the first time we kissed in your gazebo, that when a man's cock lengthens and broadens, it means the man is mere minutes away from pushing his cock between your legs."

"Yes, and you can be assured I wanted to. Instead, I came in my trousers at the same time as you came with my finger inside of you. My pants are now wet."

"How wet?" She couldn't help her very giddy, feminine smile.

"Rather wet." His piercing blue eyes twinkled.

"Do you need a washcloth?"

"I do." He pressed his cheek to her cheek, half chuckling and half groaning in her ear as he did. "You are a very wicked woman."

"I am now."

"You were glorious in your passion too."

Her cheeks flushed with heat and he lifted his head and met her gaze. "Don't be embarrassed. You drove me wild with your response to my touch. I adored it."

"Could you lift up a little?"

"I'd rather not."

"You're too heavy."

"Poor you." Another chuckle, then he popped a kiss on her lips and pushed to his feet. "It seems I must oblige you now. I wouldn't wish to flatten you when I am so very fascinated by all of your sweet curves."

"My sweet curves thank you for the relief." She pushed her skirts down, righted her nightgown and drew the neck ties together. Indeed, he did have a very large wet patch staining the front of his trousers.

He limped across to her side table, his leg clearly bothering him and she wriggled under her covers and plumped her pillows, while he poured water into the basin and dipped the cloth and wrung it out. He unbuttoned his trousers, pushed the damp cloth inside and cleaned himself. Goodness. She should turn her gaze away and not gawk while he saw to his ablutions, but she couldn't help herself, and certainly not after the precious intimacy they'd just shared. Finished, he fixed his trousers and buttoned his shirt before crunching on a button as he walked back to her.

"I'm so sorry. I'll sew your jacket buttons back on if you like."

"No, I'd rather you didn't. That jacket shall never hold buttons again, just so I'll never forget this night." He sat on the edge of her bed and faced her, his blue gaze intense. "I'm certain Tidmore is the one."

"We're to elope tomorrow night, during the masked ball."

"Is he truly the man you want as a husband?"

"How can you even ask that after the way we just kissed and touched?"

"He gave you a rose."

"I offered you a daisy, which you declined." She pushed a finger into his chest, right over his heart. "You've not asked me to marry you either. In fact, you've stated unequivocally until this moment that you've no desire for a wife. Have you changed your mind at all?"

"Yes."

"Pardon?"

"I said yes."

"Then why did you choose Lady Ashley over me when you first returned from the front line?"

"At the time, I had no desire for such a union between us. You're Harry's little sister. When you were only a few hours old, I sat in your parents' drawing room and held you bundled in my arms. Six, I was at the time, only a year on from when I'd suffered the loss of my own parents. You were so small and innocent. At that moment, I considered you my sister too. I vowed to always watch over you."

"So this, you being here in my chamber, is you watching over me?"

"Yes, and no. You've turned my world upside down, Ellie Marie. You've dragged me out of my self-exile with your decree that you're to run away with another man, and I can't allow that to happen. You've forced my hand."

"I've forced no one's hand." She gasped, shocked and outraged.

"I wanted to remain in seclusion, but now because of you, I no longer can."

"Oh, trust me, I've no intention of forcing you to offer for me."

"That's not what I meant."

"You told me once before, that you neither wanted my sympathy, worry, or interference. The same goes for me." And here she'd thought he actually might hold tender feelings for her. Instead, she'd forced his hand and that hadn't been her intention at all.

"Lady Ellie?" A knock on her door, Penny's soft whisper drifting through. "Is all well? I heard some strange noises."

"No, everything is not well, Penny." She heaved out of her bed and pushed the drapes open. She shoved a finger at the window. "You can't be found in here, Your Grace. You must go."

"We haven't finished our conversation."

"I understand exactly where this conversation is headed. After what just transpired between us, you'll no doubt feel honor bound to ask for my hand, and well, I'm not accepting any proposal other than the one I've already accepted."

Another rap at the door.

"Damn it, Ellie."

"Leave." Another jab at the window.

"You are one very stubborn woman, and we shall speak again first thing in the morning, right after I've requested your hand from Winterly. I will make you my wife." He nabbed his jacket and greatcoat and whisked away out her window.

No, he wouldn't make her his wife. Not if she had her way.

Chapter 17

Ashten had been furious with Ellie after he'd climbed out her window, had decided he'd needed to rid himself of his frustration and fury before returning home. After imparting instructions to Watts to maintain a vigil at the Trentbury's home, that he would return in the morning to speak to Winterly, he'd ridden out of town then charged hard across the wide fields of the countryside and only once he'd exhausted his anger, had he finally turned around and ridden back to Blackgale House. Now with the dawn sun close to rising, he dismounted and handed his reins to his stable hand just as Watts galloped in.

"Your Grace." Watts launched himself from his saddle.

"What's happened?" His footman would never have left his post outside Ellie's driveway unless an emergency had arisen.

"Lady Ellie, she"—he hauled in a staggered breath, half bent over and winded from his fast ride—"she left the house not long after you did."

"What do you mean she left?" His heart stopped and he thumped his chest, got it beating back into line again.

"She had Harry's carriage brought forth from storage at the rear of the property. Her driver left with her ensconced inside. No maid, although her maid had left earlier in a hack. I wasn't sure what was about, until I followed Lady Ellie. She met up with her maid who'd arrived ahead of her at Mr. Tidmore's residence. He too had a satchel packed and stepped into Harry's coach. The maid remained behind, all tearful and begging her lady to take her with her to Gretna Green. Lady Ellie declined her maid's offer and instructed the lass to speak to her sisters and inform them that she'd brought her leaving forward. She handed her maid a note to pass on to her brother as well."

"I can't believe this." How could Ellie leave him after their passionate encounter last night, before he'd even had a chance to make a formal offer of marriage for her hand to Winterly? His stallion was exhausted and would never maintain the pace he needed in his chase of his wayward lady. He bellowed to Rhodes, "Saddle two horses. I need to ride out immediately. Gorman!"

Gorman hurried across the front lawn all a fluster. "What do you need of me, Your Grace?"

"William, pack me a satchel with all that I'll need for a journey out of town, for yourself as well. Lady Ellie has run away with Mr. Tidmore and we must find her, then ensure she is brought back home to Blackgale House." He bounded inside to change his sweat-soaked clothes, Gorman hard on his heels. "I have myself a bride to catch, my future bride."

"It'll be a delight to join you, an honor and a privilege."

Ashten passed Dorothy, his housekeeper. "Fetch some water and fill my bath. Make it quick."

"Yes, Your Grace." In her aproned skirts, Dorothy, his groomsman's wife, rushed toward the kitchens calling out for two of the lads to bring pails of hot water to his chamber.

Inside his room, he shucked his boots then sent the rest of his clothes flying, while Gorman packed clothing into a satchel across the other side of his room.

The lads arrived, poured warm water into the tub before the fireplace, then he dunked down and scrubbed himself clean with a bar of soap. He dried off, donned the deep blue jacket and buff breeches Gorman had left on the bed for him, then muttered fiercely under his breath.

When he caught up with Ellie Marie, he was going to throttle her.

Chapter 18

What an endless day it had been stuck inside Harry's carriage as it had bumped along the country road toward Gretna Green. Ellie's mood had dropped further and further into despair with each hour that had passed, and all because she'd had no willpower where Ashten was concerned. Thank goodness she'd seen the error of her ways in time and had sent him on his way. Now, after so much time had passed with her being alone in Tidmore's company on the road, she no longer had a choice but to speak vows with him, because if she didn't, both she and her family would surely become the talk of all the evil gossipmongers.

"You're very quiet, Ellie." Across on the padded seat, Tidmore frowned, a deeply worried crease furrowing his brow. "If you've changed your mind, all you need to do is tell me."

"No, I will never change my mind. I'm so sorry. I don't mean to worry or upset you. I'm simply quiet because so much is about to change and my thoughts are all askew." Such guilt besieged her too. She desperately wished to clear the air between her and Tidmore, to admit her indiscretion with Ashten since the man before her would soon be her husband and he deserved to know that she'd allowed another man's touch the night before.

"Why don't you tell me what thoughts are most askew? We Americans don't always adhere to the hard and fast rules of

Society, so if you wish to speak openly and honestly with me, I would be most glad that you did." He stroked his jaw, his gaze assessing. "Is this about the duke?"

"Yes." She twisted her fingers in her lap.

"A burden shared is a burden halved."

"That is very true." Tidmore had also given her the opening she needed, and no more could she withhold what she'd done. She cleared her throat and began. "Certainly, it pained me to see Ashten place himself in isolation these past six months, and to bear witness to the ugly rumors circulating about him, particularly when I've always held such a girlish fascination for him. In my youth, he was rather like a hero to me."

"In what way?"

"He saved my life once."

"This is a tale I need to hear. How exactly?"

"Mama had warned me time and time again never to get too close to the edge of the river bordering our property with Ashten's, but one morning from my chamber window I'd spied Ashten and Harry slinging their fishing poles over their shoulders then tramping down to the river. The moment my governess turned her attention to Sophia and Olivia, I slipped out of the house and followed them to their favorite fishing spot. Ashten had set his pail and pole next to the sweeping boughs of an elm tree, while Harry had trekked a little farther around the bend upstream. I'd been so thrilled to have made my escape and I skipped along and well, the recent rains had made the embankment soggy and I slipped in a mucky spot. I went down, under the water, could barely kick back up, then Ashten was there. He'd dived in after me, then kept us both afloat as we bobbed downstream in the fast-flowing water. Where it pooled to one side, Ashten kicked us to safety and I'll forever owe him my very life. I was eight at the time."

"Has this girlish fascination continued into adulthood?"

She needed to be completely honest with him, so she

nodded. "Yes."

"In what way exactly?" He leaned back against the royal blue padded seat and crossed his legs, his forest green Cossack trousers loose about his legs and tucked into calf-high boots. His black velvet jacket sat folded on the seat beside him, the silver buttons gleaming in the last rays of the day filtering through the window.

"We've kissed, rather recently." Her chest tightened at her admission. "I'm sorry."

"And your decision about this kiss with him?"

"He made my heart race."

"I see." He coughed, then waved his hand in a continuing motion. "Is there anything more?"

"I still hold my innocence. That I can assure you."

"I believe you, Ellie."

"Will you forgive me for the kisses I've shared with him?"

"Of course." The tension in his jaw relaxed, which relaxed her own tension. "I'm glad you've shared what's on your heart and I appreciate your honesty. I would also like to share some of my own past feelings."

"Oh, go right ahead."

"I too held a boyish fascination for a young lady in my youth. She was five years older than me, and when she wed it near broke my heart. Fourteen, I was at the time, but I'd been fascinated with her for nigh on six years. That being the case, I do understand what you've said."

"What was her name?" She adored his honesty, and his declaration made her feel far less guilty.

"Elizabeth Montgomery, but everyone called her Lizzy." He turned his gaze to the window and watched the darkened trees whizzing by, the forest rising high both sides of the wooded road they traveled. A minute passed, maybe two, such a heaviness crossing his face.

"What happened to her?" His pain touched her heart, made

her want to comfort and soothe him.

"Lizzy passed away in childbirth." Scrubbing a hand over his face, he eyed her again. "The child perished not long after she did, a son born with her golden locks and enchanting blue eyes."

"I'm so sorry."

"I actually held her son as he took his last breath."

"You remained close to her after she wed?"

"Yes, particularly since Lizzy married my eldest brother, right after she'd fallen in love with him."

"Oh my." He would understand her better than anyone else could. He'd held desire for another who hadn't reciprocated that desire.

"Yes, but I did my best to never let on to her about my feelings, and from the day she wed Trevor, I became like a brother to her in every way. She was filled with love and life, an effervescence that I've never seen in a young woman since, that is until I met you."

"You and I, we have a great deal in common."

"That we do, which was why when you told me of your distress regarding Ashten and bringing him out of his self-exile, I was reminded of Trevor. He too raged with guilt over the death of Lizzy and his child, even though he wasn't to blame. My brother closed his door and wouldn't allow any of my family entry, not even my mother, not for a full twelve months. That's when I decided to sneak in and haul him out of his enforced isolation and back into the world."

"As I did with Ashten?"

"Yes, and now you've shown the duke the light at the end of the tunnel and he's sought the sunshine again. He's not only accepted there was naught he could do to save the lady who perished, but he's also left his self-exile behind. His decision to join Winterly and I in our next business venture is proof of that."

"In the future, there will never be anything more than

friendship between him and I. I can assure you of that." A promise she'd forever keep. "I give you my word."

"I believe you, but more than that, I trust you."

Now she needed to uphold that trust in every way.

She wouldn't disappoint him.

Chapter 19

Ashten rode like the blazes, Gorman racing behind him. Ellie could have chosen two or three different routes to reach Gretna Green, but he expected she'd chosen the fastest, a familiar route too since his duchy lay on the other side of these thick woods, Winterly Manor rising just beyond that.

"There's another carriage up ahead," Gorman bellowed as he galloped beside him. "This is an invigorating ride, Your Grace."

"It certainly blows the cobwebs out." He couldn't tell if the carriage was Harry's, not with the dark of the night closing in, and drat it all, but Ellie had been alone with Tidmore in Harry's coach for eighteen hours, a blasted long length of time in which they might have even consummated their upcoming marriage vows. That thought had his gut twisting.

Up ahead, the rattling of the carriage's wheels over the dirt and stone road rumbled louder with each horse length he gained on the coach. So close. He dug his knees into his horse's flanks and spurred the beast on. Atop the conveyance, the driver's shadowy figure became clearer, as did the four horses drawing the carriage. Misty air billowed as the beasts snorted, although the animals would be tiring, a rest needed for certain and the King's Inn, which sat within his duchy, was close.

As the coach broke free of the woods and the rolling fields

lay spread before them, he finally drew even with the coach door. The familiar crest of Harry's personal insignia gleamed in the rising moonlight, a coiled rope circling the initials of Harry's name. To Gorman, he yelled, "I'm going to join Lady Ellie and Tidmore, so watch my horse for me while I do, then have the driver pull over at the inn up ahead."

"Of course." A salute from his man.

Ashten hauled the door open and without any hesitation, jumped.

He landed heavily on his bad leg then rolled across the floor between the bench seats.

Ellie screamed and Tidmore dived on top of him, gripped his shoulders then shook his head as he got a better look at him. "Is that you, Ashten?"

"Yes, and I do apologize for the way I've bounded in, but I've heard there's to be an elopement, one I completely and wholeheartedly disagree with."

"Thomas, let him up." Ellie, her face ashen, fluttered a hand over her heart, her lacy wrap slipping from her shoulders. "What are you doing here?"

"Are you hurt at all?" Her pale pink day dress held a streak of dust across the front.

"No, but I've never seen you act so recklessly. Are you hurt?" She straightened her silk bonnet. "Why didn't you just ask our driver to pull over? Smithy would have recognized you and done so."

"It was a matter of urgency, and I was out of my mind with worry." He had no other excuse. Mad, he most certainly was.

"Here, up you get." Tidmore pushed to his feet and held out his hand.

"If I managed to throw myself in here, I'll manage to get back on my feet."

"As you wish." Tidmore eased back onto his seat across from Ellie and frowned at him. "I intend on speaking vows with

Lady Ellie as soon as we reach Gretna Green, and no one is going to halt that from happening."

"You must at least allow me another attempt at changing her mind."

"The lady will always have the right to choose who she wishes to wed, but I won't have her made to feel uncomfortable with any possible tongue lashing." Tidmore waved him to continue, which grated on Ashten. Perhaps the man was certain he'd never be able to change Ellie's mind, thus why he was happy for him to speak his peace.

He heaved to his feet, dusted off his buff breeches and sat on the bench next to Ellie. He took one deep, stabilizing breath. "I've had Watts keeping an eye on you, and after you left your home and collected Tidmore, he informed me of what was afoot."

"Nothing new is afoot. I already told you of my intention to elope."

"Yes, but not until the night of the masquerade, which is in full swing right now I might add. I've been forced to race across half of England to catch up to you."

"I didn't ask you to follow me."

"Listen to me, Ellie." He caught her arm, such pain washing through him.

"No." She glared and wrenched her arm free. "I'm well aware of your thoughts and that—"

"You are a cheat and a coward. That's what you are."

"I—I—" She gasped, shock and outrage flaring across her face. "How could you say such a thing to me?"

"We kissed, and you ran."

"You chose to pursue Lady Ashley over me."

"I didn't realize the depth of my feelings for you until now."

"And what feelings would those be?"

"Anger for one."

"Oh, wonderful." A snide answer, one she broke off with a huff. "I have never been so angry at anyone in my whole life either. You're an ungrateful wretch, Your Grace."

"Yes, but I'm your ungrateful wretch."

"Not anymore. Mr. Tidmore is an honest and trustworthy man, the man I intend on marrying." She lifted her dainty nose and arched a brow at him. "He gave me a rose."

"You gave me a daisy."

"You declined it, said you had no need for a daisy right now, and I've taken you at your word."

"You were well aware that I intended on returning to speak to Winterly, that I intended on asking for your hand, and you ran away instead."

"I would never force your hand."

"I wanted to be forced."

"Oh, please." The carriage slowed and rolled into the front drive of the King's Inn. Smoke puffed from the chimney of the quaint stone building ringed with night-shrouded trees.

Tidmore cleared his throat and stood. "Well, now that you've both gotten your feelings out, how about we alight from this carriage, stretch our legs and enjoy some hearty food. The horses need to be changed and then we can continue on our way."

"A superb idea, Thomas." Ellie smiled broadly at the man who Ashten wished he could hate, except Tidmore was too damn nice and an immensely honorable man as well.

"Allow me to escort you inside." Tidmore opened the door, stepped down onto the gravel driveway and extended a hand to Ellie. "I'll secure a room for you, so you can refresh yourself. Does that sound suitable?"

"It certainly does. Thank you for thinking of my welfare, Thomas." Ellie shot Ashten a narrow-eyed look over her shoulder, one that silently stated, *And that's what I expect of a gentleman.* "You are an absolute dear, Thomas," she murmured to Tidmore as she stepped onto the gravelly ground beside him.

A superb idea, Thomas. Thank you for thinking of my welfare, Thomas. You are an absolute dear, Thomas. Thomas flipping this, Thomas flipping that.

Ellie was going to send him insane, as well as into a reckless and thoughtless idiot before this day was done. Perhaps he was already halfway there. He certainly had been too forthright with her since he'd bounded into her carriage, but that was due to the fact that time was running out and he needed to change her mind. The possibility of losing her had scrambled his usually well-ordered thoughts.

Perhaps he simply needed to lay out the facts one by one and see if she could argue against each of them. He'd bring her around to his way of thinking, that she was meant for him and no one else, certainly not Thomas Tidmore, Captain Poole, or even the blasted town crier if he came calling.

He stepped down from the coach, closed the door and searched for Gorman.

Two lively children darted out from under an apple tree at the side of the inn and tore toward the stables with an apple in each hand, twin girls with identical braids and flushed cheeks.

Around the coach, he limped. A stable lad of no more than fourteen aided Ellie's driver in tending the carriage's horses, and his butler emerged from the dark atop his horse, the reins of his own steed in hand.

He crossed to his man, his leg aching like the devil.

"Do you have need of your cane?" Gorman bounded from his mount, unstrapped his cane from the saddlebags strapped to his horse and handed it to him, clear worry flaring across his face.

"Cease worrying about me, and only worry about the fact that I've yet to convince Lady Ellie to halt this nonsense of hers. She still intends to travel to Gretna Green and speak vows with Tidmore."

"What do you need me to do?"

"The lady will be taking a room to refresh herself, and that's the only time I can possibly speak to her alone. Can you distract Tidmore for me? Keep him busy, and I'll do whatever must be done with Lady Ellie."

"At once." Gorman handed the reins of their horses to another lad who dashed forward from the stables, then he thanked the lad and hurried toward the front door of the inn. Gorman opened the door, stepped aside and gestured for Ashten to enter first.

He marched inside, stomped the dirt from his boots on the mat inside the entrance and searched the main room. Tidmore and Ellie stood to one side near the fireplace warming their hands before the fire, while Thomson, the innkeeper, turned the coals with a fire poker.

Across to the crinkly-eyed proprietor, Ashten walked, his resolve firm and his cane tapping over the stony floor. "Good evening, Thomson."

"Your Grace, welcome home." Thomson slotted the poker into the iron holder and brushed his hands against his trouser-covered legs. "The wife has mutton stew cooking and the fire is blazing a real treat. Choose a table and I'll have ye served."

"My thanks, Thomson. First though, Lady Ellie is after a room to refresh herself."

"One moment. Maggie!" Thomson yelled over his shoulder.

A flush-faced woman with long strands of brown hair trickling free of her top knot tottered out of the kitchens, the swinging door swaying behind her as she wiped her hands on the brown apron tied around her ample waist. A stricken look crossed her face as she caught sight of Ellie. "Oh, my lady. Ye look exhausted and yer face is so pale."

"I'd adore a room to freshen up within." Ellie smiled at her wide.

"That ye do, for certain. The chamber ye usually freshen up

in when ye're passing through is all yours. The first door on the second floor. I'll dish ye up some stew and hot bread and bring it to the corner table." Maggie slapped Thomson on the arm. "Ye, my husband, must cease bellowing my name too. How many times must I tell ye that?"

"Once more should do nicely." A cheeky grin from Thomson.

"Thank you, Maggie. The room would be greatly appreciated." Ellie stepped back and bumped into Ashten.

"I'll escort the lady to her room." Ashten caught Ellie's hand and threaded it through his bent arm. Ellie's eyebrows pulled together in a fierce scowl, but thankfully she didn't argue with him but instead allowed him to steer her up the side stairs leading to the second-floor landing. Doors led off either side of the passageway and Ellie released his arm with a huff and marched inside the chamber Maggie had said was hers.

He ached for her, all of him, and if he could, he'd bundle her up in his arms and simply hold her close. She was his world. She always had been, and he damn well wished he'd recognized it sooner.

"Pierce Luke Blackgale." She tossed her wrap and reticule on the large bed, planted her hands on her hips and doubled the intensity of her scowl. "Explain your abominable behavior right now."

Chapter 20

Never had such anger and frustration pummeled through Ellie as it had done since Ashten had thrown himself into Harry's coach. If he'd lost his footing and tumbled under a carriage wheel rather than fallen inside, he could've been killed by his brash actions. "Tell me the truth. Why did you call me a cheat and a coward?"

"Because you've cheated me out of the chance of keeping you from this elopement, and all by your cowardly decision to take off to Gretna Green almost a full day before you'd planned to." He closed the door and glared at her with eyes of a blue so hungry in color, she had to take a step back. "I haven't been able to think correctly," he continued, "not since Watts informed me that you'd stepped into Harry's coach, collected Tidmore from his home, then left your maid behind. You're running away from me and you shouldn't be."

"Do I need to remind you of what my family will have to endure if I don't follow through with this elopement?"

"I understand the rumors will be rife." Raking one hand through his dark hair, he paced the room before her. "If you wed Tidmore, he'll take you far away from England."

"Tidmore has promised me that we'll live here half the year."

"And your heart truly tells you to choose him?"

She shoved one finger into his chest, her frustration exploding. "You've never held the same feelings for me that I've always held for you, and up until this day, you've stated unequivocally that you'll never take me to wife. I won't force your hand."

"I fear losing you." He searched her gaze. "As I already appear to be doing."

"I've now made my bed, so to speak, and must sleep in it." She strode past him to the side table, shakily lifted the jug and poured water into the basin. She plucked a washcloth from the pile and dipped it into the water, then dabbed her face and neck, her skin flushed with heat from their argument.

She tidied her hair as best as she could with the brush, retied her silk bonnet with the aid of the small hand mirror and faced her nemesis once more, the man still standing firm and tall in front of her.

"Do you love me?" Gruff words from the only man she'd ever loved.

"No, I hate you right now."

"Don't say that." He closed in on her, slowly lowered to one knee and groaned as he rubbed his bad leg.

"Pierce, what are you doing?"

"I'm proposing to you." He scrunched his face, his scowl fierce as he laid his cane on the floor beside him. "Which I'm apparently stuffing right up."

"No, I won't allow you to propose to me simply because you feel obliged to." She couldn't bear it if she'd forced him to offer for her. Their marriage would be off to a terrible start, possibly so bad she might never be able to repair it.

"And I can't allow you to wed Tidmore." He thumped one hand on his chest. "Marry me, Ellie. Not him. You wouldn't have to leave your family if you chose me. Our town and country properties are close, not separated by a wide ocean. When Harry returns on leave, you'll be here and not in the Americas, and best of all, you'll be able to argue with me daily if you wished to. I would surely allow it, as much arguing as you needed to do."

"So, you consider me an arguer, do you?"

He arched a brow, then frowned. "I'm terrible at proposals."

"It is the worst proposal I've ever had." Still, he'd chosen to offer for her when he hadn't needed to, and she had to at least thank him for that. She cupped his cheeks in her hands and looked into his eyes, her very soul twisting in on itself. "Your Grace, I do wish you well for the future and hope you find a bride you truly love and wish to wed."

"You're wishing me well?" He spluttered and cane in hand, pushed back to his feet. "Do I need to kiss you disrespectfully until you concede to my proposal?"

Oh dear. If she allowed him to kiss her in that fashion, she'd never want him to stop.

She needed to end this argument now and leave. A perfectly sane idea. She grabbed her wrap and reticule, rushed out the door and hurried downstairs.

"Ellie Marie!" Ashten pounded after her.

She skidded into the main room, rather unladylike, then brushed her pale pink skirts and straightened her lacy wrap. Wooden screens separated the central tables where travelers partook of the hearty stew and jugs of ale. Soft conversation filled the roomy space, the latticed windows overlooking the surrounding trees and fields of lush grass bathed in moonlight. The meandering length of the river which snaked through the land reflected the twinkling of stars. Ordinarily, she enjoyed stopping here while traveling to Winterly Manor, this inn within the boundary of Ashten's duchy, but tonight anxiety alone consumed her. Ashten had gotten down on one knee and proposed to her, one of her secret desires finally realized, only his proposal had not only come too late, but had also come from the forcing of his hand. She charged across to Tidmore seated in a corner booth, three bowls of mutton stew already on the table and the hearty aroma of the meat wafting to her. She smiled gallantly. "That smells divine."

"The Duke of Ashten is right behind you and appears rather mad." Tidmore stood and offered her the seat next to his, his next words whispered in her ear, "Is he all right?"

"No, he's still quite angry about my decision to elope with you, but pay no heed to him. I simply frustrate him, immensely, and I likely always will." She sat as Ashten clomped toward them.

"Our discussion is not over," Ashten blasted as he flipped the tails of his deep blue jacket and dropped into the seat across from her.

"How about we all put our frustrations aside and simply enjoy this meal?" Tidmore offered as he too returned to his seat.

"The only concession I will make right now is to have your agreement that I accompany you both to Gretna Green." Ashten continued to glare at Tidmore. "Surely you can't deny that Lady Ellie requires a chaperone for the remainder of her trip, and I am her brother's dearest friend and have known her since she the day she was born. I can act as a suitable chaperone."

"Ashten!" She wasn't having that. He wasn't suitable, not in the least. "We've already ridden this far without a chaperone, and I don't—"

"Good, it's settled then. I'll ride with you and your betrothed. Gorman and I will be your witnesses when you speak vows. You do need two witnesses, in case you weren't aware." He shoved the basket of bread in the center of the table under her nose. "Care for some bread, my wee daisy."

"No, thank you, and I am not *your wee daisy*." Yet she snatched the bread, tore a hunk off and jabbed it into her stew. She bit into one end then moaned at the delicious juices trickling over her tongue. "Oh my, this is a very tasty stew. Maggie has outdone herself tonight."

"Maggie does make the finest mutton stew in all of England." Ashten spooned a mouthful between his lips and moaned too. "I missed breakfast and luncheon, so I do apologize if I act the hog right now."

"Then we shall both be hogs together for this is the first meal I've partaken of all day as well." Ellie couldn't suppress her giggle, her anger at Ashten sliding swiftly away, as it always had in the past after he'd riled her. He could charm her with one single word and this time it had been "hog." She truly did adore him. He was here because of his worry for her, which she couldn't fault him for, terribly misplaced proposal and all. She reached across the table and touched his arm. "I'm sorry for saying I hate you."

"You're forgiven."

"You're supposed to apologize too." She kicked him under the table and he grunted.

"I apologize, and I believe I'll leave it at that. I've no wish to get myself into any more trouble tonight."

Tidmore chuckled as he glanced between the two of them. "This all sounds suspiciously as if you two just made up?"

"We have." She motioned to Tidmore's legs. "Which leg do you favor for future kicks?"

"None, my dear lady. I never intend to get your gander up as Ashten has done."

Chapter 21

In the early hours of the following morning, the dawn sun having just arisen, Ellie tried to block out the sliver of annoying sunshine streaming through the gap in the curtains over the coach window she sat beside. Tidmore and Gorman slept across from her, their heads propped against the backrest of the coach, their eyes closed and chests rising slowly but surely. Beside her, Ashten sat with his eyes open, staring straight ahead, just as he'd done each time she'd peeked at him during the night.

Slowly, he turned his gaze on her, then said not a word as long minutes passed. Such sorrow fisted her heart and wouldn't abate. Why couldn't she have just said yes to Ashten's proposal and not worry over why he'd issued it? Hmm, that's right. Because she didn't wish to take advantage of him. Keeping him for herself would have been selfish.

Breaking their eye contact, she leaned her head against the side of the coach and closed her eyes. All her life she'd always been able to rely on Ashten, just as she had with Harry. He'd even saved her the day he'd dived into the river and held onto her until they'd neared the shallows farther downstream. He'd always been a huge part of her life, and she couldn't imagine a time when he wouldn't be around if she absolutely needed him.

"We've butted heads often over the years." Whispered words in her ear, Ashten having moved closer, although she kept her eyes closed. Gently, he tucked a lock of her hair behind her ear, his fingers soft against her skin and his voice lowering further as he said, "I'm certain we always will."

She remained quiet. Answering him wouldn't be helpful.

"You and I have always belonged together, and I wish I'd seen that sooner." He grazed a knuckle across her cheek. "It scares me to think I might not be able to convince you of my sincerity in time. Yet I have every reason to fight for you, and mark my words, I shall."

Goodness, but this man could capture her heart with his words when he wished to. Still, she kept her eyes closed and her resolve firm.

"I can't return to London without you, Ellie, or go on as I did before. I need to be able to hold you close, to be surrounded by you and your family. I never wish to let you go, and it's beyond time that I finally followed my heart and accepted the truth between us."

Oh, he was laying on the charm now. She also knew the truth, and it wasn't what he'd just said. Clearly, he'd dug in his heels, his determination to change her mind, intense.

"I wish to seek out adventures with you, to always be at your side and for you to be at mine, for every day that's to come. I wish to raise a family with you, to give you children and your mama grandchildren."

She needed to remain strong and not allow him to sway her mind. She had her family to think about, Thomas Tidmore too, and she'd given her word to Thomas that she'd speak vows with him. Never had she gone against her word before, and she didn't intend on starting now. Yes, because to do anything else, would be to place her family in a terrible position.

She drifted toward sleep, Ashten's soft lips brushing the top of her head, his touch soothing her as nothing else ever would.

Damn the man.

Chapter 22

The snorting of horses echoed within Ellie's head first, then as she stirred, she sensed the absolute quiet and cessation of movement. The coach had come to a complete stop at some point and she stretched and pushed her eyes open. Her slippered feet, now tucked under a blue and white patchwork blanket, were propped on the bench seat and she lay sprawled across it with no one else about.

Gritty eyed, she balled her fists and rubbed them until she'd worked the crusted sleep free. The warmth of the late afternoon sunshine seeped in through the open coach door, along with the delightful pine freshness of the forest. The twittering of birds drew her outside and she searched either side of the dusty road lined with a thick copse of trees.

"Lady Ellie." Smithy waved at her from atop the driver's seat, his shirtsleeves rolled to his elbows and his thick gray coat folded beside him. "It's a lovely afternoon."

"Yes, it is, Smithy. Where is His Grace?" She adjusted her lacy wrap.

"Check with Gorman." He hoisted one thumb over his shoulder. "Other side of the coach."

"Thank you. I shall." With her pale pink skirts in hand, she trekked around the tail end of the coach and walked across the lush grass within a small meadow. Gorman sloshed a pail of water between the horses tethered to a tree. The coach's geldings had been removed from their harnesses and now munched on the grass along with Ashten and Gorman's steeds. "Good afternoon, Gorman."

"Afternoon, my lady." Gorman, now dressed in sandy colored trousers and a black vest over a white shirt, set his pail down and crossed to her. He eyed Smithy and instructed, "Pass the lady's valise down, if you will."

Smithy dropped the valise and Gorman caught it.

"If you wish to change," Gorman murmured as he led the way across the meadow, "there's an abandoned woodsman's shack just through the trees. I gave it a sweep when we arrived, removed the dust and the cobwebs."

"You brought a broom with you?" She followed Gorman as he led the way into the woods and twenty feet in, a woodsman's shack indeed appeared through the trees, one with a thatched roof and wooden beamed sides.

"No, but I fashioned a rather good broom out of a long thin branch with a pine bough knotted to it. His Grace changed inside and declared the spot safe and secure for you as well, once you'd awoken of course. Smithy and I were instructed to allow you to sleep for as long as you needed." A heave against the door, and Gorman set her valise inside and held the door open for her to enter.

"Where would His Grace be right now?" She stepped inside the windowless shack, the remains of a straw mattress falling to bits along one wall, although the straw had been nicely scooped in front of it and the makeshift broom propped in one corner. Indeed, not one cobweb swung from the rafters.

"He took some line down to the river from Smithy's box, intends on catching some fish for dinner."

"Oh, I see." No matter he was a duke, her Ashten had always enjoyed fishing. He thrived on being outdoors, his very soul as one with nature itself. It was where he came alive, and always would.

"Call out once you've need of me again." Dipping his head as he backed out the door, Gorman left.

She waited at the door until Gorman had disappeared back toward the meadow then she snuck out and found the perfect bush to crouch behind. Done with her ablutions, she walked into the shack and perused the clothing Penny had packed for her. She selected a walking dress with heavier burgundy skirts and long snug sleeves which would provide more warmth as they traveled farther north toward their border with Scotland. She added a velvet wrap of the same deep burgundy shade, tugged her riding boots on and closed her valise. Outside, she stuck two fingers in her mouth and whistled, just as Harry had taught her to do as a child, and as no lady should ever know how to do.

At the shrill call, Gorman emerged through the trees, his lips lifting as he trotted back, the streaks of silver at the sides of his dark head glinting in the late afternoon sunshine. "The duke's mother could whistle loud and clear, just as you've done. It does my heart good to hear such a whistle from a lady again."

"What was she like, Ashten's mother?"

"The duchess was a rare beauty, like a butterfly with glowing, near translucent wings that sent her soaring high or dipping low. Every sweet and radiant flower she touched bloomed even brighter because of her fingers upon it. She adored all those at Blackgale Park as well, would visit the villagers within their duchy, spend time with the families of the servants, whether they were from the household staff or the outdoor staff. She enjoyed tending the flower beds with the gardener, would wander through the huge stables and feed apple slices to the horses, and of the three-hundred staff at her beck and call, she knew each and every one of us by name."

"I wish I'd known her."

"You are so very like her, both in your sweet nature and fierce spirit."

"Thank you, that is a huge compliment." One she adored. "Gorman, I'd like to speak to His Grace if you can show me the way to where he's fishing."

"Absolutely, I'll escort you to the river then I'll see to the return of your valise to the coach. His Grace certainly wouldn't appreciate it if I allowed you to walk about unattended on your own. Mr. Tidmore either."

"Oh my, yes, where is Mr. Tidmore?" Good grief. She'd not once thought of her betrothed since she'd awoken.

"The gentleman is also fishing, although a little farther downstream from the duke. The two are enjoying a competition as such."

"To see who can catch the most fish?" Whenever Ashten and Harry had gone fishing, they'd bet on who could bring home the most fish, the winner receiving a prize from the other, of whatever they'd chosen as the stakes.

"Yes, that is correct." Gorman led the way through the trees and she followed. Within a hundred feet, the trees thinned and she stepped into another small meadow with lush grass lining both sides of the river, fast-flowing water cascading over rocks and splashing around the bend.

Ashten stood on a rock jutting out from a mound of rocks, his fishing line in the water and a pail beside him, the tail ends of a few fish poking out. His navy breeches hugged his tight backside to perfection, the cuffs of his billowy white shirt rolled back a few inches to expose the crisp hairs on his forearms. He'd discarded his jacket and cravat, which sat folded in a tidy pile on the bank, and of which Gorman swiftly collected then disappeared with his armful along the trail they'd just traversed.

She moved closer to Ashten, taking care not to squish the daisies waving from within the thick grass. Merriment twinkled in his piercing blue eyes as he turned and caught sight of her, although he said not a word, but instead smiled wider. Sometimes one didn't need to say a word to understand what another was thinking, and his smile certainly conveyed his current thoughts, that he was once again in his element, at home with nature where he most desired.

As his line got tugged, he turned his attention back to the water and dragged in another fish. It bounced from the end of his line as he brought it up onto the rocks. He crouched, tugged the hook free and dropped the fish into his pail, his leg not appearing to be bothering him at all as he strode back across the rocks with barely a limp. He set his pail down at the water's edge, scooped a handful of sand and scrubbed his hands clean before dunking them again and washing the sand away.

Over the tops of the trees, the sun dipped lower, the afternoon almost at an end, but not yet. She wished to collect some of these sweet daisies waving their heads within the grass. She fashioned a makeshift bowl in her skirts by pinning together the velvet at the front, then plucked as many daisies as she could and wandered back to Ashten, who had remained watching her with a slightly silly grin on his handsome face.

"Are you going to make me a daisy chain?" The look of hope on his face was impossible to miss.

"That all depends on who caught the most fish."

"Hopefully me. I just hooked my fifth fish. Don't let go of your skirts." Gently, he cupped her cheeks in his hands, his smile smoldering as he pressed his body so close to hers.

"What are you doing?"

"Wishing you a good evening, since the night is almost upon us."

"You're touching me."

"Yes, and if Gorman weren't within shouting distance and Tidmore fishing just a little farther down the river, I would instead be toppling you onto the ground and kissing you as disrespectfully as I possibly could."

"Then I should go and see how my betrothed is."

"It's interesting that you've come to see me first." One

wicked smirk.

"I'm simply taking the chance to say a fond farewell to my brother's dearest friend while I can." She reached up on her toes and kissed his cheek. "There truly is no need for you to chaperone us to Gretna Green."

"There is every need, my sweet ray of sunshine." He wrapped his arms around her waist and dipped her back off her feet, a smoldering look flickering in his eyes.

"What are you doing? I'm going to drop my daisies." She fumbled to keep them contained.

"How many children would you like to have?" He licked across the seam of her lips.

"Ashten." She opened her mouth to growl him further, only he groaned and covered her mouth with his. He kissed her, so sweetly and passionately and her world tilted.

"I'd like five," he murmured against her lips as he eased back an inch. "The same number of children as what you have in your family. I've always thought that a good number. There aren't too many siblings as to get under one's feet, yet also not too few that one can't have at least one brother or sister close at hand if needed."

"You told me you have a remote third cousin who shall inherit your title and lands upon your death, that he will do fine enough as your heir."

"I've changed my mind on that front."

"No, you are still attempting to change mine, and your ploy won't work."

"Ellie!" A shout echoed through the trees, Tidmore's shout.

Oh goodness. She wriggled out of Ashten's arms, thankfully without dropping her daisies. She breathed deep and tried to compose herself just as Tidmore strode through the thick foliage with a welcoming smile.

"There you are." He waved with one hand, his other gripping his pail. "Did you have a good sleep?"

"Yes, and thank you for allowing me to continue resting after we stopped to water the horses." She pecked his cheek. "How many fish did you catch?"

"Four." He tucked a loose lock of her hair behind her ear, then arched a brow at Ashten. "What about you, eh, Duke?"

"Five." A rumbling growl, Ashten's jovial mood now at a clear end.

Thank heavens for that. An angry Ashten was far easier to deal with than a determined Ashten.

Chapter 23

Ashten paced before the crackling fire Gorman had lit, where his man had skinned and cut the fish he and Tidmore had caught before propping the meat over a rack to cook above the flickering flames. Smithy sat on a log he'd pulled up to the fire, and was currently whittling away on a piece of wood, fashioning it into the shape of a puppy by the looks, one strikingly similar to Beast. He nicked out tiny ears and added a wagging tail. Yes, definitely a replica of Beast.

The last of the sun's rays lit the sky a streaky red, then the sun sank and the night closed in fully around them. Stars twinkled, dazzling the eye, although nothing could ever truly dazzle him more than the woman seated on the blanket before the fire. Ellie had crossed her legs under her burgundy skirts, her hands busy as she carefully threaded her daisy chain together. His daisy chain. He'd won it fair and square by catching more fish than Tidmore.

Tidmore sat close to her, his brown trouser-clad legs kicked out and crossed at the ankle, his gaze fastened on Ellie's creation. His new business partner, a man he both admired and hated, still stood in his way of capturing Ellie back, and right now his window of opportunity was dwindling by the hour. He needed to make tonight count—which he would.

"Lizzy used to make daisy chains." Sad, yet softly spoken

words from Tidmore.

"She did?" Ellie raised one perky golden brow.

"Yes, and she used to gift them to my brother. I pinched one of them once." The man's gaze softened, as if memories had surged forth this night. "I placed it inside the pages of one of my favorite books. I still have it."

"Who's Lizzy?" Beyond curious, he couldn't withhold his question.

"Thomas's sister-in-law," Ellie answered him as she threaded another daisy into place. "Lizzy married his older brother, only she passed away in childbirth."

"Oh, I see." He cast his gaze to Tidmore. "I apologize and offer my sincere condolences. Was the loss recent?"

"No, but sometimes it feels so."

"Yes, the loss of loved ones isn't easy, no matter how much time has passed." Even though only five when he'd lost his parents, at times it felt as if it were yesterday when he'd waved farewell to them from the front step of Blackgale Park. Certainly, he had no intention of losing any more of his loved ones, and that included Ellie. Somehow and some way, he'd make sure she was his by the end of this excursion to Gretna Green. No other outcome, could he allow.

"The fish is cooked, Your Grace." Gorman served the grilled fish on a large platter he'd procured from the locked box atop the coach and set the dish on the blanket where everyone could reach it.

Ellie selected a morsel first and popped it in her mouth. "Mmm, superb." She cast an adoring gaze at Tidmore. "That piece must have been from one of the four fish you caught."

"After that compliment, I certainly hope it was."

She giggled and Ashten settled himself on the blanket, his thoughts tumbling into a terrible mess. He ate and filled his belly while the moon rose higher and glimmered brighter. If only his ability to secure Ellie to his side remained as equally as bright.

Unfortunately, with each minute that passed, she drew farther and farther away from him, as if his advances frightened her.

Not over his dead body would he ever allow his Ellie to give another man what was his, which included all of her, heart, body and soul. Things needed to change, this very night. He'd begin by speaking with Tidmore, since his attempt at changing Ellie's mind hadn't altered their current position. He pushed to his feet, collected his cane and eyed his new business partner. "I'd like a word with you in private, if I may?"

"Of course. I wouldn't mind stretching my legs one last time before we set out. Gretna Green awaits."

"Yes, it does." He clasped Smithy's shoulder as he passed the driver. "Harness the horses and ready them for leaving." To Gorman, he muttered, "Ensure Lady Ellie is settled in the coach. Tidmore and I won't be long, and we'll leave as soon as we return." Done dispersing his orders, he scooped up the daisy chain Ellie had completed and looped it around his neck and with his treasure, walked into the trees toward the river with Tidmore at his side, the moon lighting their way.

Once he reached the water's edge where he and Ellie had kissed, he turned to the man who currently called Ellie his bride-to-be and drew in a deep breath. "I'm not sure how to say this, Tidmore."

"You love her." Tidmore crossed his arms, his legs planted wide. "It's clear to see, old chap."

"I do, deeply, but she'll never change her mind about marrying you unless you step down."

"I understand what it's like to lose the one you love." Tidmore's jaw tensed, yet compassion shimmered in his eyes. "I can also see the love you hold for her, and which she holds for you in return."

"She'll continue to set that love aside, particularly since she's given you her word that she'll speak vows with you once we reach Gretna Green. Ellie is loyal, and you currently hold her loyalty." He thumped one hand against his heart. "I can't live without her."

"I'm aware that you've followed us for that very reason, even though she hasn't yet come to that conclusion." Tidmore stared up at the night sky, then eyed him again. "I'd also be a fool to steal her away from you, to try to recreate the love you two hold and claim it for myself. I'd be doing none of us a favor if I did."

"Then I have your agreement, that you'll step down?"

Tidmore said nothing for one excruciatingly long minute, then slowly, his business partner clapped him on the shoulder. "I have a better idea. Do you wish to hear it?"

"I certainly do."

Chapter 24

Another three full days passed and they'd made good time reaching Dumfries and Galloway, near the mouth of the River Esk. The old blacksmith's shop at Gretna Green shone like a beacon at the end of the road where it forked, the village rising beyond it and smoke curling into the air from the stone houses. So many runaway marriages had occurred here, where couples could join together legally provided they had two witnesses to oversee their ceremony. Ellie prayed one of the anvil priests would be ready and awaiting their arrival this night, her vows with Thomas Tidmore mere minutes away now from being spoken.

She straightened her white skirts, the empire gown her chosen wedding attire, which she'd changed into at their last stop. The neckline was low, the bodice fitted and the skirts flaring from the high waist. With her white lacy shawl draped over her shoulders, she donned her white gloves and cast her gaze out the window again. Candles burned in the front latticed windows of the blacksmith's shop, the odd leafy tree surrounding the building shimmering in the moonlight.

Smithy knocked on the top of the coach. "We're here, Your Grace."

"That we are." Ashten opened the door as the coach halted in the wide circular driveway, then he bounded down and set the footstep platform in place. He looked so smart in his tailed black jacket and fine black trousers, his white cravat knotted and her daisy chain still looped around his neck—the tiny yellow flowers having dried, their petals curled inward. He held his cane in one hand and extended his other hand to her. "You look beautiful."

"Thank you." Gently, she placed her hand in his, alighted from the carriage and accepted Tidmore's arm as he alighted down too. Her future husband led her up the front steps after Ashten, who knocked on the front door for them.

"Not much longer now before we're wed," Tidmore whispered in her ear. "How are you feeling?"

"My heart is pounding so fast." A little woozy again, she rested a hand on Ashten's back where he stood in front of her and the moment she did, her head cleared a touch. His warmth penetrated through to her, then as the door swung open, she fisted his jacket to halt him from stepping inside.

"Welcome to ye all. Come in, come in. Ye be the third couple who've arrived this night." A beaming blacksmith dressed in buckskin breeches and a black tunic with a dusty leather apron tied around his waist, motioned them inside, his shoulders as wide as the doorway itself and his legs like tree trunks.

Ashten offered her his arm as well and she grasped ahold of his forearm like a life line.

"Everything will be all right." Ashten kissed her cheek then spoke to the anvil priest. "I'm Pierce Luke Blackgale, the Duke of Ashten, and with me is Lady Ellie Trentbury." He motioned to Tidmore and Gorman. "Mr. Thomas Tidmore, and Mr. William Gorman."

Ellie surveyed the main room while Ashten spoke in the blacksmith's ear. It was cozy and warm, a fire burning in the corner and various tools hanging on the walls and from hooks over a wide workbench. The anvil, a heavy steel block with a flat top, concave sides and one end pointed, took pride of place in the center of the room, that particular tool being the one which the blacksmith used to hammer his metal into shape and which she'd soon be speaking her vows with Thomas before.

"I see ye've got two witnesses, Your Grace." The blacksmith placed a bible beside his anvil and metal hammer, then set out a piece of parchment and wrote on it, a document she and Thomas would need on their return as proof that their wedding had taken place. "Do ye both come here of yer own free will?"

"We do," all three men answered him, rather than just Thomas himself. Strange, but fine. It was good for her witnesses to have stated their acceptance of being here too.

"Good, good." The blacksmith eyed her. "And ye, my lady. Do ye come here of yer own free will?"

"I do." Her hands shook and her knees wobbled, so she tightened her grip on Ashten and Thomas's arms as they stood either side of her.

"You're doing fine, Ellie." Tidmore gave her hand a reassuring squeeze.

"Do ye take this man to be yer lawfully wedded husband?" the blacksmith asked her.

"I will." Although wasn't he supposed to ask Thomas that question first? Oh well, provided they were asked the same question, that's all that mattered.

"Do ye take this woman to be yer lawfully wedded wife?" the blacksmith asked Ashten.

"I will."

"Wait, Pierce, no." She shook her head at the blacksmith. "I'm supposed to be marrying Mr. Thomas Tidmore, not the Duke of Ashten." She pointed at Thomas to make her point clear. "Him."

"That's not what the duke just told me." The blacksmith blinked, eyed Ashten, and at Ashten's wide grin, the blacksmith broke into a beaming smile. "Verra well, Your Grace."

"Verra well what?" she screeched, and she never ever screeched.

"I see I'm right, and you, sweet lass, are wrong." The blacksmith picked up his hammer and with a merry voice, bellowed, "I hereby declare that Lady Ellie Trentbury and Pierce Luke Blackgale, the Duke of Ashten, are hereby man and wife. In the name o' the Father, the Son, and the Holy Ghost, it shall be. I wish ye both a wonderful life together." He slammed the hammer down on the anvil, the loud clang ringing in her ears and echoing out the open window.

"You did that on purpose." She shoved one finger into Ashten's chest, all anxiety gone and only anger thrumming in its place. "You, you, you—wait." She turned on Thomas and jabbed his chest too. "Did you know that was going to happen?"

"You're just like my Lizzy, loyal and generous, and loving everyone around you and needing to be there for them. I understand your feelings for me are far different to the feelings you hold for Ashten and I could never take those feelings away, particularly when the duke holds you in such great esteem." Thomas grasped her hands. "No matter how long we have on this great Earth, we must take ahold of love when it comes our way and keep it close. Ashten loves you, and I won't stand in the way of that kind of true love." He motioned to Ashten, who stood with an excited grin on his face. "You may kiss your bride, Your Grace."

"Don't you dare." She wanted to take a swing at both men and lay them down flat. "I should have been consulted over this change in wedding plans."

"Then let me consult you now." Pierce caught her around the waist and whispered against her lips. "I love you, more than any man could ever love a woman, and now I get to call you my wife. Consider yourself shackled to a man who intends on loving you ruthlessly for the rest of your life."

"Release me now."

"No, I'm never releasing you again, my sweet ray of sunshine." He covered her mouth with his and kissed her, so fiercely and so passionately that she had no hope but to respond.

Pierce had stolen her heart as a child, had never returned it in all these years, and yes, she loved him more than her next breath. She kissed him back, while Tidmore and Gorman raised the roof with their cheers.

"Are you still angry with me?" Pierce asked her, his mouth a whisper from hers.

"Yes, why didn't you tell me you loved me before now?"

"I thought it was obvious."

"No, it wasn't." She slapped his chest.

"Wait, my love." He caught her hand before she could slap his chest a second time. "Are we having our first argument as man and wife?"

"I'd say this is our second argument, and a great deal of groveling will be required if you wish to mend both of those arguments."

"That I can do, along with a great deal of disrespectful kisses too." A twinkle in his beautiful blue eyes. "Do you agree?"

"Yes, that I most definitely agree with." She grasped his lapels and drew his mouth back to hers.

He was hers, forever, and never would she let him go again.

Chapter 25

"I can't believe this is happening." Ellie twined her fingers with Ashten's in the privacy of the room they'd taken at the Gretna Green village inn. "What do we do now?"

"We consummate our marriage by joining together as one." Gaze smoldering, he dipped a finger along the low neckline of her white empire gown, her wrap draped over the corner chair where he'd tossed it and his jacket as they'd walked in. "Come closer, my sweet."

"I'm already close enough." Yet she swayed forward, her hips now touching his hips.

"That's better." He captured her lips in a scorching kiss, his body a fierce stamp of heat that pounded warmth into her.

"Perhaps we should douse the fire." It blazed in the hearth at the end of their four-poster bed, the light of the golden flames flickering all about. "I'm already too hot."

"My wife," he murmured against her lips. "It's less clothes you need to be wearing if you wish to cool down, not the fire doused."

"You are becoming more domineering by the minute."

"I simply want my wife naked and underneath me." He tugged the puffy capped sleeves of her gown down to her wrists and grinned as her arms got trapped at her sides, her breasts bobbing free. With his blue gaze lifted to hers, his eyes swimming with hunger and need, he whispered huskily, "It's time for bed."

"Free me first."

"Perhaps later." He clamped her bottom and kept her tight against him then dipped his head and sucked one of her nipples deep into his mouth. "You're so beautiful. Tell me if I go too fast, or if you're frightened at any point. If you are, I'll slow down."

"You could never frighten me." She leaned into him, his erection thrusting upward and tenting his fine black trousers. Desperate for more, she rubbed her hips against his hips, the hard length of him searing her skin through her gown. "I believe I might like fast."

"You're so tasty," he moaned and drew her nipple deeper into his mouth.

Wicked and wanton tingles raced through her body and even though her arms were still trapped, she managed to wriggle one hand up high enough to cup his cock through his pants.

"Ellie Marie." He hissed, his shaft jerking in her hand. "Clearly, I will have to keep my eyes on you."

"Please do, and your mouth as well." At her naughty words, his shaft lengthened even further, the tip now protruding from the waistband of his trousers underneath the hem of his shirt. A small wet patch glistened on the linen. "How is it that you keep growing, and how much bigger will your penis get?"

"It's about at bursting point now, and never fear. We will fit together as a man and wife do, which will be perfectly. He lifted and carried her to the bed, then carefully slid her onto the soft brown fur covering, scooped her breasts together and licked across both nipples. The raspy stroke of his tongue across the sensitive tips sent a bolt of heat streaking straight through her core and she gasped for breath.

"Pierce?"

"I'm going to undress myself now." He gave her no more

warning as he eased onto his knees, pressed them into the mattress either side of her hips and unknotted his impeccably tied cravat. He tossed it across the plump white pillows propped underneath the headboard then unbuttoned his shirt and let the linen fall gently through his fingers onto the bed.

She desperately wished to caress his glorious chest, to follow the trail of dark hair disappearing below the waistband of his trousers, to touch every firm and unbending inch of him. "You must release me. I wish to touch you."

"Soon." He slid back down overtop of her, rubbed his chest over her incredibly sensitive breasts and made her moan.

"I need you."

"I need you too," he whispered as he eased up onto his elbows, gripped the loosened waistband of his trousers and shoved the black fabric down his muscled legs and off. His cock stood at full attention and brushed his belly, the rounded head darkening to a shiny raspberry color before her eyes.

Good gracious, he'd said he would fit inside her, but she wasn't entirely certain of exactly how. Trust him though, she would.

"What's going through your mind right now, my delectable wife?" He nudged her legs apart, lifted her gown's white skirts to her upper thighs and knelt between them, his balls drawing tighter and higher into the nest of dark brown curls springing around his shaft.

"I—" She squirmed a little, wriggling upward and higher toward the pillows, her hands slipping free of their bonds.

"No, remain right where you are." He caught her ankles, dragged her back down, her skirts rucking up to her waist and exposing her most private parts. He feasted his gaze on her below then trailed one finger through the golden curls covering her entrance. "Have no fear. This part of you here is where I long to be, snuggled deep inside you."

"I'm anxious, but more because I've always wanted to be

your wife. These past few days I've been pushing you away for your own good." A myriad of emotions tumbled through her, love the strongest of them all. She squeezed her eyes shut, this moment one she'd been waiting so very long for.

"Look at me, Ellie."

She opened her eyes and breathed slowly in and out.

"I see you've managed to free your hands. Touch me if you wish. I need to feel your hands on me, to know you want me as much as I want you."

"I'm not sure which part of you I want to touch first." Although she began with his delicious mouth. She ran her thumbs across his divine lips, which were made for kissing, then she stroked down his neck and swished over the hard planes of his chest. She adored all of him, even his injured leg where a long scar cut through the flesh of his upper thigh. Breathless, and a whole lot dizzy, she murmured, "I love you, Pierce. Thank you for sabotaging my wedding and making me your wife."

"I never would have allowed you to wed Tidmore. I love you, and I apologize that it took so long for me to realize the truth and come after you. My heart is yours, will always be yours." He lifted her feet, pressed them into the mattress and spread her knees wider. Gently, he massaged her inner thighs, kneading with delicious strokes all the way to her groin. "It's time for you to relax. Set your elbows down and rest back on the bed. Think only of how much I want to love you, of how I wish to give you the ultimate pleasure, with my hands and my mouth."

"Whatever you do, may I do to you in return?" Head on the pillow, she placed all her trust in him, just as she'd always done through the years.

"Later. Much later." He eased onto the bed between her thighs, hooked her legs over his shoulders until her bottom lifted off the bed and she lay fully exposed to him.

"Oh goodness." She slapped her hands over her eyes.

"You're beautiful, deliciously pink and lush looking. I can't wait to press my mouth here and—"

"Wait. What?" She flung her hands away.

"I told you to relax." He chuckled then grinning, parted her folds and plunged one finger deep inside her. She jumped as pleasure ricocheted so fiercely through her and hardened her nipples into tight points, her gown wrapped around her waist and her hands fisted in the fur cover. "I see you like that. Are you ready for more?"

"No—yes—no."

"I believe you are." He stroked her harder and faster, rubbed his thumb across her nub until she arched into his touch.

"More." She couldn't halt her plea.

Another finger, two now working a sweet magic inside her, stretching and filling her, then he dipped his head and licked her flesh in the most intimate way, with both his wicked fingers moving in a deep and delicious rhythm. Every flick of his tongue and drive of his fingers had her climbing higher, the sensation building to a peak that she had nowhere to go but to soar from.

"Pierce?" Her body splintered, her core rippling with wave after wave of pure bliss.

"They'll be a pinch of pain, but I promise it won't be for long." His words washed over her, her mind and body still somewhere far away in that glorious place he'd taken her to.

Chapter 26

Ashten didn't wish to hurt Ellie, not one bit, but so too he didn't wish to be parted from her another moment longer. He would join them together and make her his wife in every way. With one more stroke of her below, he gripped his shaft and rubbed the head over her slick folds. He wanted to make her come, over and over until she couldn't breathe for the pleasure. He gorged himself on her full breasts, then her pouty mouth until she moaned against his lips and kissed him just as ferociously in return.

Yes, it was time. No more could he hold on. With his hands on her hips, he lifted her higher to accept his full length, then as she arched into him, he pushed against her barrier, tore through her innocence and plunged deep inside her.

"Oh my." She sighed against his lips as he kissed her, then she hooked her legs around his hips, clutched his butt and pulled him in even deeper. "Mmm, it is as you said. You belong here, snuggled deep inside me."

"Yes, my love, as I always will." He lifted up, then slowly pushed back in. "Come soar to the heavens with me. I want to join you there this time."

"It's such a beautiful place." She cupped his face in her hands and kissed him. "I could get rather addicted to flying there with you."

He pounded harder and deeper, then got lost as her inner muscles tightened and dragged him in even further. He kissed her with all the love he held within him, his release exploding powerfully along with hers as she came a second time, and deep within his wife, he spilled his seed and prayed it would take ahold. He wanted a family with her, one as loving and loud as her own family was, and he wanted to hold his wife and children close to his heart for the rest of his life, to never be alone again, but to share all that he was with her.

"My heart is yours," he whispered against her lips.

"I never knew this moment could be so wonderful." Hands buried in his hair, she brought his mouth back to hers and kissed him with a seductively sweet kiss that stirred his cock back to life. "Thrilling too, like when one races across the fields on horseback."

"You could ride me if you wished." He wanted her atop him, had been envisaging her doing so for days. "Ellie, now that your body has accepted mine, when we join together as one, we can enjoy a multitude of various positions." He kissed her and she kissed him back, with an excitement that said he'd certainly tweaked her curiosity. His wife was so incredibly alluring with her golden eyes that shimmered with love, her beautiful creamy skin and luscious pouty lips.

"I can truly ride you? How is that even possible?"

"You need to be seated over my hips while I'm lying below you."

"Interesting." She raised a quizzical brow. "And you don't mind having an adventurous wife who wishes to ride you, in your bed that is?"

"Your adventurous nature is what I adore the most about you."

"Then how do we make this switch?"

"Allow me." He rolled them both over.

"That was quick." She giggled as she straddled his hips

proper from atop, his cock still buried deep within her. "You are a man of action."

"I didn't care to wait a second longer." Every inch of her glorious body caught the flickering firelight as she wriggled against his groin, his cock disappearing deep into her slick channel. She lifted up a touch, her breasts swaying heavy and full, her rosy nipples making his mouth water in his desire to devour them.

"Am I doing this right?" She lifted and exposed an inch of his shaft, then gently ran one finger around the base and gasped.

"Lift up a touch higher, Ellie."

She did, exposing another inch of his cock.

"Higher still."

Another inch, her finger sliding over her slick essence coating him.

"Now lower yourself until you're fully seated again."

She sank down on him with excruciating slowness, her breath quickening and her eyes rolling as she moaned her approval.

"Did you like that?" Slowly, he grazed a finger from between her breasts to her belly, then trailed lower and swirled through the golden curls covering her entrance. With a gentle swish, he rubbed her nub.

"Mmm, oh yes, and you feel incredible inside of me." Back arched, she covered his hand and held his fingers in place against her nub as she lifted again and lowered back down. "Your fingers are magical."

"I adore touching you."

"Then please, don't stop." She eased up again, slid her hand around his exposed cock then let go and sank back down on him.

With her breasts bobbing right in front of his face, he shoved his elbows behind him and latched his mouth over one nipple. He nipped it with his teeth, then licked and sucked on it.

Her breathing stuttered, her smile so wicked. "I believe I

shall enjoy riding you, Your Grace."

"I believe I shall enjoy it more." He gripped her hips, lifted her then dropped her back down harder. "Ride me as fast and as furiously as you wish. I promise I shall enjoy every second of it."

"Are you certain?" Peeking through her long lashes, she built her pace, lifting and lowering, faster and faster, her back arched and breasts thrust out.

He groaned. "I'm positively certain."

"Then I'm riding you correctly?" She reached behind her and cupped his balls.

"Hell, yes." He jerked at her incredible touch.

"This is a beautiful way to make love." She caressed both his balls, then built her speed until she was flying across the fields with him.

He aided her where he could, holding her hips to keep her in place and his cock hardened impossibly further as her sweet channel tightened so beautifully around him. Such seductive torture, of the kind he wished to endure for the rest of his life. He stretched out under her, a shimmer of heat blazing at the base of his spine and ricocheting around to the front. Damn, he wouldn't be able to hold on much longer. He flicked her nub and she sucked in a harsh breath, her belly tightening and her torso shaking.

"I feel too much." She lifted up again, her channel accepting all of him as she came back down on him.

"So do I." He flicked her nub a second time and she cried out his name, her body convulsing over his.

Blood pounding, his cock hammering at him, he accepted all of her as her inner muscles squeezed his flesh in the most delicious of ways. He thrust his hips higher to catch every last contraction and she sank ever deeper over him. With his balls tightening, he pounded and she bucked overtop, his cock deep in the heart of her, right where he belonged.

"You're my wife, always mine," he growled as he came in a

hot rush.

"Mmm," she murmured as she slowed her pace, her eyelids drifting down. She slumped on top of his chest, her smile so content. "Yes, I'm always yours."

He tucked her close against his heart, beyond content with her in his arms. Never could he imagine his life without her, and now he no longer had to.

Together, forever entwined, he drifted toward sleep with the woman he loved held securely within his arms.

She was the only woman who'd ever stolen his heart.

The only woman who'd ever hold it too.

Chapter 27

Inside her husband's bedchamber at Blackgale House in town a month later, Ellie gripped Pierce's shoulders as sweet pleasure coursed through her. Sheer happiness and peace invaded her heart, the man connected as one with her as equally at peace as she was, and she sensed that to the very depths of her soul. Their bond had strengthened and tightened these past few weeks as they'd enjoyed a very long honeymoon on their journey back from Gretna Green. Three weeks they'd spent at Blackgale Park before returning to London a week ago.

"What are you thinking, my sweet?"

"That Gorman must be wondering if he's to ever see us again." She also needed to do more than just send another letter of apology to her family for missing yet another family dinner. "Also, Mama will descend on us before too long if we don't drop by."

"Then I'll lock the front door. I'm certainly not leaving this bedchamber until I've gotten you with child." Smiling wickedly, he snuck a gold silk ribbon from under his pillow and caressed it across her skin, down her back and over her bare bottom as she laid overtop of him.

"Is that the ribbon you pocketed after pulling me from the river?" Surely, he hadn't kept it all these years? She'd never forget the moment when he'd removed it from her bedraggled locks after saving her life so many years ago.

"Yes, and it's always been my good luck charm. Wherever I go, this ribbon goes. I even kept it in my shirt pocket, close to my heart, while in the hussars."

"If you'd told me that before now, I would have known you loved me." Her heart clenched with the deep love she held for him. "By the way, my courses are late, by a fortnight, and they're never late."

"Are you telling me I've already gotten you with child?" He cupped her breasts in his hands and nuzzled them, his husky voice rumbling deep in his throat and vibrating against her sensitive mounds.

"Yes, that's what I'm saying."

"Perhaps we should make certain." Gently, he rolled her over onto her back beside him, then smoothed one hand across her flat belly, a sensual grin lifting his lips. "And I mean by making love again."

"Making love with you again sounds perfect."

He was all she would ever desire in a husband, and she'd be forever grateful to Thomas Tidmore for stepping aside and allowing her to wed the man she'd always loved and adored. Her bond with Ashten was one that had sprouted in their childhood, had bloomed through to adulthood, and which now overflowed her heart.

She kissed her new husband again, falling ever more deeply in love with him.

He was the man who'd first stolen her heart, and the man who would forever hold it.

To sweet love, gold ribbons, and daisy chains.

May they be present in their lives, for all time to come.

JOANNE WADSWORTH

The Earl's Bride

~ COMING NEXT ~

Regency Brides Series, Book Two

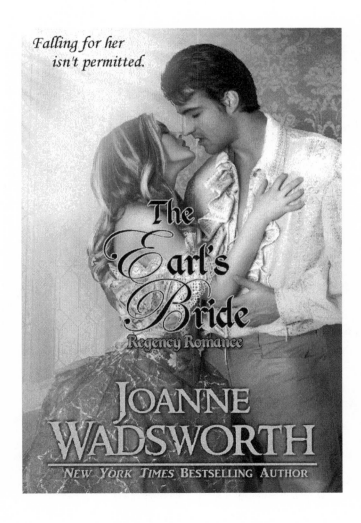

Falling for her
isn't permitted.

The Earl's Bride

Regency Romance

JOANNE WADSWORTH

NEW YORK TIMES BESTSELLING AUTHOR

Regency Brides

The Duke's Bride, Book One
The Earl's Bride, Book Two
The Wartime Bride, Book Three
The Earl's Secret Bride, Book Four
The Prince's Bride, Book Five
Her Pirate Prince, Book Six
Chased by the Corsair, Book Seven

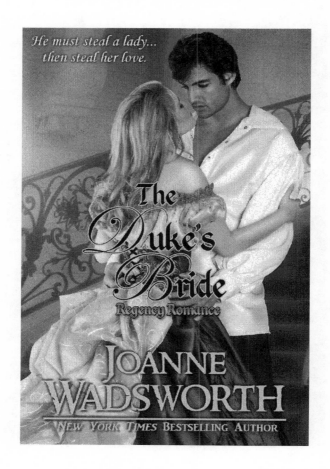

The Matheson Brothers

Highlander's Desire, Book One
Highlander's Passion, Book Two
Highlander's Seduction, Book Three

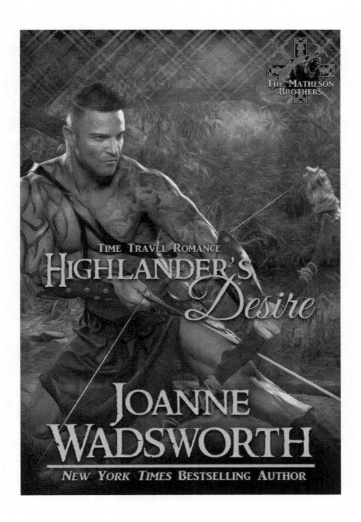

The Matheson Brothers Continued

Highlander's Kiss, Book Four
Highlander's Heart, Book Five
Highlander's Sword, Book Six

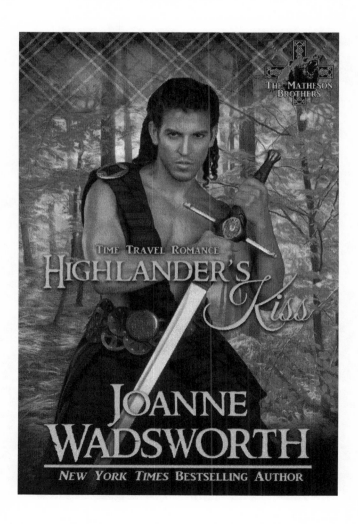

The Matheson Brothers Continued

Highlander's Bride, Book Seven
Highlander's Caress, Book Eight
Highlander's Touch, Book Nine

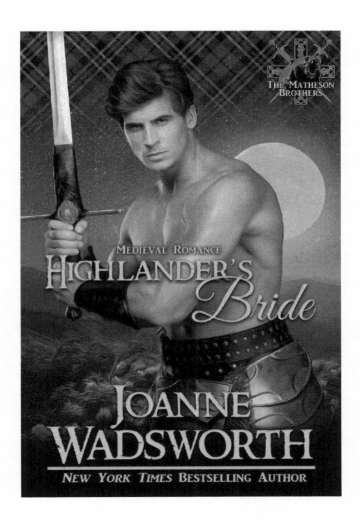

The Matheson Brothers Continued

Highlander's Shifter, Book Ten
Highlander's Claim, Book Eleven
Highlander's Courage, Book Twelve
Highlander's Mermaid, Book Thirteen

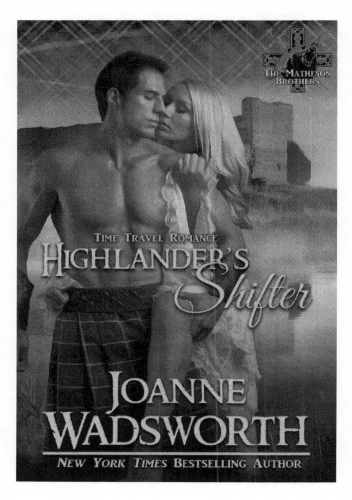

Highlander Heat

Highlander's Castle, Book One
Highlander's Magic, Book Two
Highlander's Charm, Book Three
Highlander's Guardian, Book Four
Highlander's Faerie, Book Five
Highlander's Champion, Book Six

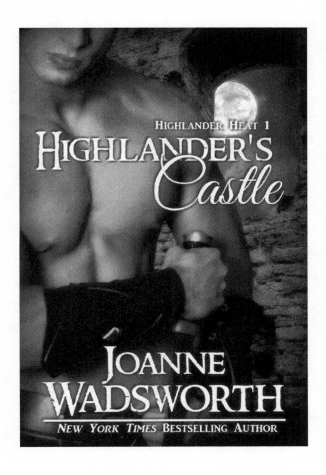

Princesses of Myth

Protector, Book One
Warrior, Book Two
Hunter (Short Story - Included in Warrior, Book Two)
Enchanter, Book Three
Healer, Book Four
Chaser, Book Five
Pirate Princess, Book Six

JOANNE WADSWORTH

Billionaire Bodyguards

Billionaire Bodyguard Attraction, Book One
Billionaire Bodyguard Boss, Book Two
Billionaire Bodyguard Fling, Book Three

JOANNE WADSWORTH

Joanne Wadsworth is a *New York Times* and *USA Today* Bestselling Author who adores getting lost in the world of romance, no matter what era in time that might be. Hot alpha Highlanders hound her, demanding their stories are told and she's devoted to ensuring they meet their match, whether that be with a feisty lass from the present or far in the past.

Living on a tiny island at the bottom of the world, she calls New Zealand home. Big-dreamer, hoarder of chocolate, and addicted to juicy watermelons since the age of five, she chases after her four energetic children and has her own hunky hubby on the side.

So come and join in all the fun, because this kiwi girl promises to give you her "Hot-Highlander" oath, to bring you a heart-pounding, sexy adventure from the moment you turn the first page. This is where romance meets fantasy and adventure...

To learn more about Joanne and her works, visit
http://www.joannewadsworth.com